Loveswept ®537

Janet Evanovich
Naughty Neighbor

BANTAM BOOKS
NEW YORK · TORONTO · LONDON · SYDNEY · AUCKLAND

NAUGHTY NEIGHBOR

A Bantam Book / April 1992

If you would be interested in receiving protective vinyl covers for your Loveswept books, please write to this address for information:

> Loveswept
> Bantam Books
> P.O. Box 985
> Hicksville, NY 11802

ISBN 0-553-44152-3

Published simultaneously in the United States and Canada

PRINTED IN THE UNITED STATES OF AMERICA

OPM   0 9 8 7 6 5 4 3 2 1

"This is a good place to park," Pete said, stopping the Porsche a few yards down the road from the farmhouse. "It's dark and secluded. We won't be seen."

Louisa shivered as he caressed a tendril of her hair. He had wonderful hands, she thought, strong and sensual. She felt herself succumbing to the intoxication of the moment, falling victim to the physical attraction she felt for Pete. She figured that the car was the perfect setting to engage in an exploratory kiss, that a person couldn't make a big mistake in these cramped quarters. "Well," she said, her voice husky and slightly breathless.

Pete felt the temperature in the car rise. "Well," he replied, unsure what to do next, afraid if he moved too fast his fantasy-come-true would pop like a soap bubble.

Louisa curled her fingers into Pete's jacket and pulled him within inches. He looked like a kid who'd been told he could have ice cream for dinner and didn't believe it. "So," she said, "all smoke and no fire, huh?"

"I was under the impression you didn't want fire."

She leaned forward until their noses almost touched. "I was under the impression you didn't much care what I wanted. This is a heck of a time to get sensitive."

He had his seat back and Louisa on his lap faster than she could formulate a protest. His hands pulled her blouse from her skirt so he could touch her heated flesh, and his mouth covered hers in a kiss that made no effort at restraint. There was fire, all right, more than she'd expected. Heat, and need, and aching desire, and she felt herself flaming out of control. . . .

WHAT ARE *LOVESWEPT* ROMANCES?

They are stories of true romance and touching emotion. We believe those two very important ingredients are constants in our highly sensual and very believable stories in the *LOVESWEPT* line. Our goal is to give you, the reader, stories of consistently high quality that may sometimes make you laugh, sometimes make you cry, but are always fresh and creative and contain many delightful surprises within their pages.

Most romance fans read an enormous number of books. Those they truly love, they keep. Others may be traded with friends and soon forgotten. We hope that each *LOVESWEPT* romance will be a treasure—a "keeper." We will always try to publish

LOVE STORIES YOU'LL NEVER FORGET
BY AUTHORS YOU'LL ALWAYS REMEMBER

The Editors

One

Pete Streeter came awake on the third ring—just in time to hear the answering machine pick up the call. Streeter knew what the message would be; he'd been receiving the same one for three days. The message came at all hours of the day and night. It was untraceable, originating from public phones throughout the city. It was cryptic. A single word. "Stop." The voice was electronic. Streeter understood the warning. He also resented it. He swore softly, more out of habit than feeling, then rolled over and went back to sleep.

Louisa Brannigan looked up at her ceiling and tried to control the anger that was bubbling inside her. It was four-thirty in the morning and the idiot upstairs had just gotten another call.

He got them all night long. Not that she cared, but her bedside portable phone picked up his signal. The phone rang a second time, sending her flying from the bed in a rage. "That's it!" she shouted. "I can't take it anymore. I need my sleep. I need quiet. I need . . ." She stood with hands and teeth clenched, eyes narrowed, nose wrinkled, but she couldn't think what else she needed, so she snatched the phone from her night table, marched into the bathroom, threw the phone into the toilet, and closed the lid. Almost at once, peace descended on her. "Much better," she said.

Three hours later Louisa opened a tired eye and stared at the digital clock beside her bed. She stared at it for a full minute before her brain kicked in and responded with a shot of adrenaline. She'd slept through the alarm. "Damn."

She hurled herself to her feet and ran to the bathroom with her red flannel nightshirt flapping around her calves. She stopped dead in her tracks when she saw the slim silver antenna caught between the toilet lid and seat. She'd drowned her phone. Raising the lid, she gingerly transferred the phone to the wastebasket. It was impossible not to reflect on the symbolism. Her life, like her phone, was in the hopper.

With no time to waste, she took a quick shower and dashed back to the bedroom, shaking her curly dark brown hair like a dog in a rainstorm. She peered into the mirror over her cherrywood bureau while she picked at her bangs and took stock: Dark circles under her bloodshot blue eyes, definite water retention, and she felt shorter than her usual five feet six. It was not going to be a power day, she decided, turning to her closet with a resigned sigh.

Three weeks earlier she'd celebrated her thirtieth birthday with lunch at the sedate Willard and a late supper at the Hard Rock Cafe. Be eclectic, she'd told herself. Go for it. This morning she wasn't feeling nearly so expansive as she pulled on panty hose and zipped herself into a black wool gabardine skirt. Her blouse was silk and matched the magenta suit jacket. Her earrings were big and chunky and gold. Her mood was dark and cranky.

She trudged to the kitchen, taking note of the grim fact that it was only Tuesday, wondering how she was going to make it through the week when the loser upstairs kept her awake all night long. She'd left polite notes on his front door. She'd called the rental office. To date, she'd avoided confronting him face-to-face. She knew it was a fault. She had problems with confrontation. She was aggressive, but she wasn't assertive. She was a wimp. The admission dragged a groan from her.

The truth was, her problems ran deeper than lack of sleep. She had a monster job that was growing more unwieldly with each passing day. In the beginning being press secretary to Senator Nolan Bishop had meant clipping news articles and keeping his calendar in order. Recently, he'd changed his profile to high, and the office staff was scrambling, trying to adjust to the pressure-cooker atmosphere. Her hours and her responsibilities had doubled. Her new role was exciting, but she was much more tense. Her personal life was nonexistent.

She dumped a handful of beans into the coffee grinder, punched the grind button, and took pleasure in the simple act of smashing something into miniscule pieces. She was developing violent tendencies, she thought. "Today coffee beans, tomorrow mass mayhem," she muttered. She had to get a grip. She dropped a filter into the top of the coffee maker, added the ground coffee, boiling water, and impatiently watched the coffee drip into the glass pot. She was grossly late, but she wasn't leaving the house without her coffee. There were certain rituals that shouldn't be sacrificed. In Louisa Brannigan's opinion, a civilized cup of coffee in the morning was what separated man from beast.

She poured herself a cup and felt a stab of satisfaction when she heard the thunk of her morning paper against the heavy wood front door of the two-story brick row house. Lately, Louisa had taken to telling herself it was the little things in life that really mattered. Lunch at the Willard was nice on her birthday, but fresh sheets, perfectly cooked pasta, glasses without water spots, and five minutes to leaf through the paper before leaving for work were pleasures she could count on day in and day out. She especially loved the five minutes she allotted for the paper. Five minutes of peace and sanity. Five minutes to enjoy her coffee and read the funnies. It wasn't too much to ask, was it?

Pete Streeter also heard the paper hit. When it suited him, Streeter occupied the apartment above Louisa Brannigan's. He had his own entrance, his own on-street parking, and his own hot water heater, but he didn't have his own paper delivery. Ordinarily, Streeter didn't give a fig about the morning paper, but there was a movie review he wanted to read this particular day, so he padded down a flight of stairs and snatched Louisa Brannigan's paper.

His door clicked closed a moment before hers was carefully opened. If he'd known Louisa, he might have smiled at the colorful cursing coming from the front porch, but he didn't know Louisa, so he took himself upstairs, oblivious to the outrage he'd aroused. He spread the paper on the scarred, butcher-block kitchen table and drained half a cup of industrial strength, scalding hot sludge from a twenty-five-cup coffee urn. He grunted at the movie review and shuffled off to his bedroom for a pack of cigarettes. When he got to the bedroom, he remembered he'd given up smoking. He muttered a few satisfyingly crude phrases and scowled at his cat. Scowling at the cat was one of those gestures of habit that neither man nor feline took seriously. In truth, the cat was Pete's best friend.

Louisa narrowed her eyes and glared at the door next to hers. It was *him.* The oaf had stolen her paper. She'd never met him. Didn't know what he looked like. What she knew was that he came skulking in at all hours of the night, and that he played his music too loud. He leaked disgusting cooking smells into the heating system, left his laundry in the basement washer and dryer for days at a time, and more often than not parked his car in *her* parking space. She hated him with the sort of passion only forced cohabitation could produce. The man was scum.

She should bang on his door and demand her paper back, she thought. But what if he wouldn't give it to her? What then? She could hardly duke it out with him. He was probably large and hairy. And she couldn't prove that he had her paper, could she? It wasn't as if there were witnesses. All right, so she could do without a paper for one crummy morning. After all, she was late and probably didn't have time to read the paper, anyway. Right? Wrong. She'd allocated herself five minutes. Five lousy minutes, and the creep upstairs was reading *her* paper on *her* time. What was worse, he was getting away with it because deep down inside she was a wimp. She was afraid of the big, hairy slob who lived on the second floor. "Ugh," she said. "I hate being a wimp. I hate being a wimp!"

Okay, that does it, she told herself. She was not going to be intimidated by a man who thought fried onions and Spam were two of the four essential food groups. She thumped on his door with her fist, and then she gave it a kick. "I know you're in there!" she yelled. "And I know you're reading *my* paper!"

Pete looked up from the sports section and frowned. It was seven-thirty in the morning and some rude person was raising holy hell on his front porch. "This used to be such a perfect neighborhood," he said to his cat. "One block from the Metro stop, three blocks from the zoo, reasonable rent for Washington, D.C." He shook his head. "Now look at what it's come to . . . weirdos hammering on my door at seven-thirty in the morning." A shrill female voice carried up to him. "Uh-oh," he said, "it's the ditz downstairs, and she wants her paper." He kicked back on a kitchen chair and grinned. She was mad, and she was *not* being polite. He looked at his watch. She'd have to leave for work pretty soon. He could wait her out. "We'll let her cool off a little," he told the cat. "It's always best to avoid violent women."

Louisa gave one last kick. He was ignoring her! "Slimy, yellow-bellied coward," she shouted. "You're not going to get away with this! I will *not* be ignored!" She stomped back into her house and took the broom handle to the kitchen ceiling. *Thunk, thunk, thunk.* "This is for parking in my parking space. And this is for hogging the dryer. And this is for waking me up every night with your late calls." *Thunk, thunk, thunk.*

Pete sighed. She was becoming annoying. The floor was vibrating, and he could hear muffled shouts coming from the air duct. "I like to think of myself as a patient person," he said to the cat, "but she's starting to get on my nerves. I can't concentrate on the funnies with all this noise."

He pushed away from the table and stood, searching through his jeans for a stick of gum. When he didn't find any, he gave another sigh and ambled out of the kitchen, down the stairs to the front porch. In her haste to harass him, the woman-from-hell had left her door open, so Pete Streeter walked in and followed the racket to the kitchen. He took a wide stance, hands on hips, dark black brows drawn together, and bellowed over her thumping and shouting. "Lady, what *is* your problem?"

Louisa whirled around in midthump. "Ulk." Fury was quickly replaced with panic over the fact that there was a large, almost naked man standing in her kitchen. "Who are you? What are you doing in my house?"

"I'm Pete Streeter. I occupy the apartment above you, and you're ruining my morning with your ranting and raving." He grabbed the broom from her and threw it into the hall. "No more brooms. No more kicking my door. No more cussing at the top of your lungs." He paused to look at her. She was prettier than he'd imagined. Average height with a lean, athletic body and a classic oval face. Snappy dresser. Too bad she was such a fruitcake.

Louisa was temporarily speechless. She'd been right about him being big and hairy, she thought, but she'd been wrong about the overall effect. He was six feet, with a rawboned, tightly muscled body, low slung jeans that sat on slim hips, and the most glorious head of curly, shoulder-length brown hair she'd ever seen. It was rock-star hair. Hair she'd die for. "Is that really your own hair?" she asked.

"Yeah."

"You play in a band?"

"No. I write movie scripts."

Figures, Louisa thought, a flake from Hollywood. Her eyes narrowed. "You took my newspaper!"

"Sorry."

"I want my paper back."

"Be reasonable, I'm not done reading it, and you don't have time to read it now. You're late for work."

"How do you know I'm late for work?"

"Lady, I could set my clock by you. At five-thirty your alarm goes off. I don't know what the devil you do at that hour of the morning, but it involves a lot of door slamming. At six-thirty there's more door slamming. You take a shower, tune your radio to NPR, and force me to listen to news until you leave precisely at seven-thirty every weekday morning."

"I didn't know my noise carried up to you."

"Sweetheart, I can hear when your zipper goes down. And you shouldn't be talking to your mother about your dates. Time to cut the umbilical cord, you know?"

She felt the air stick in her lungs. "You listen to my phone calls?"

"Yeah, and it's pretty depressing. Why don't you move your phone away from the air duct—"

"Out!" she screamed. "Get out of my apartment, out of my sight, out of my life! I'm going to get Mace. I'm going to get a gun. If I ever see you again, I'll permanently disable you!"

Streeter grinned. "Must be awful to have PMS like this."

"Ugh." She smacked her fist against her forehead.

Washington was cold in February. Wind barreled up the open mall and wide avenues, and the sun hung shrunken and pale in the gray winter sky. The granite buildings seemed unrooted without their flower borders and the sere grass flattened under intrepid tourist feet. Street people huddled in plastic tents constructed over subway grates. Bureaucrats went about business as usual.

Louisa worked in the Hart Building, just north of the Supreme Court and northeast of the Capitol itself. She stretched at her desk and looked beyond the heavy teal-and-gold drapes framing windows that opened to an inner courtyard. It was six-thirty and the courtyard was dark. She was the last one left in the office, and the exodus of workers had slowed in the outside corridor. All things considered, it hadn't been a bad day.

She'd managed to keep her boss on schedule and lint-free through two luncheon meetings, an interview with a *Post* reporter, a question-and-answer session with forty fifth graders, and an afternoon tea at the Australian Embassy. She'd coerced their two interns into stuffing and stamping the monthly newsletter to constituents. She'd badgered the caterer into an affordable buffet for the spring fund-raiser. And she'd secured a slot for her senator on *Good Morning America*.

She retrieved her purse from the bottom drawer and pushed away from the desk. She buttoned her long wool greatcoat high to her neck, switched the lights off, and closed the office door behind her. She exited the building at C and 1st Street, and her attention was immediately drawn to two men arguing half a block away. One of the men was her boss, and she recognized the other as Senator Stuart Maislin. Maislin gave Nolan Bishop a jab to the chest with his finger, and Nolan went rigid, then stiffly nodded his head. Maislin stood with hands clenched for a moment, then wheeled around and climbed into the limo idling at curbside. The car pulled out into traffic. Bishop turned and quickly walked east on C Street.

Louisa was only mildly surprised. Maislin had a reputation for strong-arm tactics. He was a powerful man in the Senate, and some said he had Oval Office aspirations. It was also whispered about that he had bad friends. Louisa turned her collar up against the wind and marched across the street, pushing the incident from her mind. Sometimes a blind eye was called for on Capitol Hill.

It was past seven when she emerged from the Metro station at Connecticut and Woodley. She turned left at Woodley and walked one block to

27th Street through one of the many residential pockets in urban Washington. The sidewalks were tipped from tree roots and worn smooth from generations of baby buggy wheels, roller skates, and leather-soled shoes. Four-story-high trees grew in the dirt median between sidewalk and street. The street was narrow from curb-parked cars and bumpy with patch jobs done by the D.C. Department of Transportation. It was a neighborhood pulling itself out of midlife crises, struggling with genteel neglect. It was a neighborhood of double-income families who required close-by gourmet takeouts and same-day shirt service.

She had her head down, searching in her purse for her key, when she approached her house. She gasped when she realized there was a large dark form on her porch steps. She pressed her lips tight together when she saw it was Streeter in an unbuttoned shearling jacket with the collar turned up.

He stood and held her paper out to her. "I thought I should give this to you personally."

"Why?"

He followed her up the stairs and slouched against her door, hands in pockets, feet crossed at the ankle. "You seemed unusually bent out of shape this morning. I thought maybe there was some special significance to this particular paper. Like, maybe you're a spy and there was a microdot in the Style section."

She stuffed the paper under her arm and continued fishing in her handbag. "I'm not a spy. I'm press secretary to Senator Nolan Bishop. I was unusually bent out of shape because I was tired, and because I hate you."

"How could you hate me? You don't even know me."

She paused in her search for the key and looked up at him. "I know you well enough to thoroughly dislike you. I'd give you specific reasons, but it'd take all night, and I don't want to spend that much time in your presence."

"This is about the phone calls to your mother, isn't it? You're embarrassed because I know you aren't sleeping with the guy you've been dating for the past four months."

"Get a life."

Streeter's grin flashed white in the darkness. "Why aren't you sleeping with him?"

"He doesn't appeal to me. We're just friends."

"So, who *are* you sleeping with?"

"I'm not sleeping with—" She clamped her mouth shut and shoved her key into the lock. "It's none of your business. Get out of my way. You're leaning on my door."

Forty-five minutes later she was freshly showered and dressed in a cream-colored silk suit. She slipped her feet into a pair of matching heels, shrugged into her ankle-length black dress coat, and groaned when she caught a glimpse of the clock in the kitchen. She was late for the senator's cocktail party. It couldn't be helped. She'd had to make calls to the coast, and then she'd had to wait for the calls to be returned. She let herself out, locked the door, and almost tripped over Pete Streeter. He was back to sitting on the porch in the dark. She squinted down at him. "I almost stepped on you. What are you doing out here?"

"Sitting."

"You're very weird."

"You're not the first person who's said that."

A car turned onto the street. Its headlights flashed against parked cars as it moved forward. Pete stood and backed into the deep shadows. He pulled Louisa with him.

"Let go of me!" Louisa said. "I'll scream. I'll turn you into a soprano. I know how to do it. I took a self-defense course."

"Don't flatter yourself. I'm not interested in your body. I just want you out of the light." That wasn't entirely true, he thought, but this wasn't the time to go into detail. The car cruised by, and Pete relaxed his hold on her. He reached into his pocket for a cigarette and grumbled when he didn't find one. He searched for gum and struck out on that too.

"What are you looking for?" She was almost afraid to ask.

"Gum. I'm trying to quit smoking."

Another car rolled by, and Louisa watched Streeter shrink back against the building. "Okay, what's going on with these cars?" she asked. "Every time a car goes by you duck out of sight."

"It's a long story."

She looked at her watch. "Can you do it in thirty seconds?"

"No."

"Make an effort."

"Some yokel's threatened to vandalize my car."

"Did you call the police?"

"Yeah, and they've made two pass-bys, but they can't baby-sit my car round the clock. So I thought I'd hang out here for a while."

A dark, late-model sedan turned the corner and proceeded down the street. The car slowed and then stopped in front of Louisa's house. Louisa felt Streeter's arms wrap around her and pull her flat against him.

"Move back against the wall with me," he whispered.

The sedan door opened and there was the sound of feet shuffling on pavement. A man approached a car at curbside, raised a sledgehammer to shoulder level, and swung. There was the sound of glass being shattered. He moved quickly, smashing the windshield and the side mirror.

"Hey!" Pete yelled. "What do you think you're doing?"

A second man stepped from the sedan and leveled a gun at Streeter.

"Uh-oh," Streeter said. He threw his apartment door open and yanked Louisa inside.

Several shots were fired, and Louisa hung on to Pete Streeter as if he were life itself. Her heart hammered in her chest, and her breath refused to leave her lungs. She opened her mouth to speak but nothing came out.

Peter was having a similar reaction. He wasn't sure if it was the result of the gunshots or the fact that Louisa Brannigan had practically laminated herself to him. She had a death grip on his jacket lapels, and her leg was securely wedged between his. It wasn't an unpleasant feeling. He thought about the proximity of his bedroom and wondered how long her terror would last. Long enough to maneuver her upstairs? Probably not. Besides, she was mentally unstable, he told himself. And she wasn't his type. And she hated him. One by one, he pried her fingers off the shearling. "You're okay," he said. "You're not hurt."

"He shot at us!"

"Warning shots. He wasn't serious. He just didn't want us getting in the way while he trashed the car."

He led her to the front porch, and they stood at the top of the stairs and looked at the damage. The windshield, back window, and driver's side window had been smashed. "That's odd," Pete said. "I drive a black Porsche, and the car that's been vandalized looks like a little black Ford."

Louisa couldn't believe her eyes. "I drive a little black Ford. I had to park in your parking space last night because you were parked in mine. They wrecked *my* car."

"Bummer."

"That's the best you can come up with? Bummer? First you steal my paper. Now you get my windows pulverized. And all you can say is bummer?"

"I didn't steal your paper. I borrowed it. And I didn't get your windows pulverized. It was fate."

"It wasn't fate, you imbecile! You constantly park in my parking space! Haven't you noticed there are numbers painted at curbside? Your car belongs in the space marked ten-thirty-eight B. My car belongs in the space marked ten-thirty-eight A. It's easy to remember. It coincides with our mailing address." Dear Lord, she thought, the only homo erectus dumber than this guy was the one who'd attacked her car.

"Boy, you get uptight about the damnedest things," Pete said. "You need to relax a little."

"I used to be relaxed. I used to be well adjusted. I used to sleep nights. Then *you* moved in. You were gone for months. Why did you have to come back? You probably find it hard to believe, but there wasn't a single shoot-out in this neighborhood while you were away."

"Boring, huh?"

The man was dealing drugs, she decided. Long hair, Hollywood-type, drove an expensive car with a car phone. Next thing the house would probably be machine-gunned by some rival drug lord. Tomorrow she'd look for a new place to live. "I don't want to know any more about this," Louisa said. "I didn't see it. I'm going to pretend it never happened. I didn't like the car, anyway. It's the wrong color black."

She was babbling, Pete thought. She was on

the edge. Probably because of her lousy sex life. Abstinence did terrible things to a person's disposition. He knew firsthand because lately his sex life wasn't all that great, either. "I guess we should call the police," he said.

She looked at her watch. She didn't have time for the police. "I'll call the police tomorrow."

"Bad move," Streeter said. "If you call the police now, they might be able to catch the guys."

"Listen," Louisa said, "I'm supposed to be at a cocktail party at my boss's house right now, and if I don't show up, I'm going to be in deep doodoo. *You* call the police. You probably have lots of experience with the police, anyway."

"Hold it," Pete said. "How are you going to get to this party?"

"I'll call a cab."

Pete stood there for a moment, grappling with an odd mixture of lust and guilt. He supposed he was, to some extent, responsible for the damage to her car. He shoved his hand into his pocket and came up with a key. "That's not necessary. You can drive my Porsche."

Louisa felt her mouth drop open. *His* car? The car someone wanted to disintegrate? Was he kidding? "Nice of you to offer, but I couldn't possibly . . ."

She was reluctant to take him up on his offer because he had such a great car, he decided. She was probably afraid she'd get it scratched or something. He thought that was sweet. He took her by the elbow and pulled her down the stairs.

"Don't worry about scratching it. It already has a scratch. It's on the right front fender just above the headlight."

She dug her heels in. "I'm *not* driving your car."

He gave her a shove. "What's your name?"

"Louisa Brannigan."

He opened the driver's side door to the Porsche and settled her in.

"Okay, Lou, have a good time and try to keep your speed down. It shimmies a little at one-twenty."

"Louisa! My name is Louisa!"

"Whatever."

Two

Louisa sampled a crab puff and smiled pleasantly at Sam Gundy. The man made shoes—lots of them. And he was telling Louisa exactly how it was done.

Louisa felt her eyes begin to cross and snapped herself to attention. She took a quick peek around the room. Everything seemed to be running smoothly. Nolan was courting big business tonight, looking to replenish almost empty campaign coffers. He'd chosen his guests carefully. They were all good party members, all very wealthy, all very boring. Nolan knew better than to be upstaged when he wanted money. He always made sure he was the best dressed, best looking, most politically powerful person in the room when he made his pitch for support. And he always invited a few members of the press to his parties. It helped him achieve "star quality," he said. Nolan was big on "star quality." Nolan was a man on the way up. And Louisa knew if she did her job well, she'd go up with him.

"You ever been inside a shoe factory?" Sam asked Louisa.

"No sir, I haven't."

"It's pretty exciting."

"I bet."

Female laughter rose above the murmurings of polite society. Nothing alarming, but loud enough to catch Louisa's attention. Nolan had a small staff, and they all wore several hats. Among other things, it was Louisa's job to make sure social occasions ran smoothly. She adjusted the volume on heated arguments, poured coffee into drunks, and made sure under-the-table fondlings were kept discreet.

"I'd be happy to show you around my shoe factory if you ever get up to my neck of the woods," Sam Gundy said.

Another ripple went through the room. Something was causing a stir. Louisa's party radar clicked into hyperdrive. "If you'll excuse me," she said to Gundy. "I think I'd better check . . ."

She turned and bumped into Pete Streeter. He was wearing jeans with a hole in the knee, beat-up white tennis shoes, a black T-shirt, and a custom-tailored navy faille tux jacket. He had his hair slicked back and pulled into a pony tail. Nolan Bishop was no slouch when it came to looks, Louisa thought, but Pete Streeter made Nolan look like Buster Brown.

Pete draped his left arm over Louisa's shoulders and leaned into her. "How's it going, babe?"

Louisa swallowed audibly and put her hand to her forehead to make sure her hair roots weren't smoldering. She was blushing, hot and furious. It was a first. Too young for the change of life, she thought. What was left? Extreme embarrassment and a sexual attraction that bordered on the ridiculous. "What are you doing here?" she asked Streeter.

"Thought I'd come check up on you." Streeter turned his attention to Sam Gundy. "She's been under a lot of stress lately," he explained. He shook his finger at Gundy. "And you should be ashamed of yourself, luring a sweet young thing like this up to see your dirty old shoe factory. I guess I know what you have in mind."

Gundy sucked in his breath. "I was going to show her shoes!"

"Yeah," Pete said, "that's what they all say." He clamped a hand at the nape of Louisa's neck to prevent her from wriggling away from him. "You look all flushed," he said to her. "I bet you haven't had dinner yet."

"Crab puff," she managed. "I had a crab puff."

"You see," he said to Gundy. "She really needs someone to take care of her. It's a good thing I showed up."

A woman walked up to them. "Aren't you Pete Streeter?" she asked. "I saw your picture on the cover of *GQ*."

"A lot of people make that mistake," Pete said. "I'm not that person at all. We just have the same tailor. And it's the hair. Really," he told her. "I'm not him." He gave Louisa a friendly pat on her bottom. "Don't go away. I'll get you some food."

Louisa looked for a sharp knife, but there weren't any within reach. Just as well. It'd be a shame to ruin the tux jacket. It was a masterpiece. So was Pete Streeter, she admitted, but that wasn't going to stop her from mutilating him once they were alone.

Pete wandered over to the buffet table, took a plate, and wondered what the devil he was doing at this party. He'd told himself he was worried about the Porsche, but he knew that was baloney. The horrible truth, he decided, was that he'd had an intense, irrational craving to see more of Louisa Brannigan. It was a frightening revelation. Even more frightening was the fact that he didn't have a clue *why* he was so attracted to her. He couldn't find anything redeeming about the woman, although she didn't look bad in the silky suit. He loaded a plate with slivers of fresh fruit and a mound of tiny sandwiches. He snaked his way back through the crowd and handed the plate to Louisa. "Eat up."

"I don't—"

He popped a sandwich into her mouth. "Chew."

"Mmmmmph."

One of the media people sidled up to Pete and introduced himself. "I heard you were in town," he said. "I heard you were doing something big, something controversial."

"We'll see," Pete told him. "It's still in the research stage."

A man with a Minicam appeared from no-where and trained the recorder on Streeter. It drew more people.

Louisa felt a hand tug at her sleeve. It was Nolan. "Who *is* this guy?"

"Pete Streeter."

"What's he doing here? Did you invite him?"

"Not exactly."

"Well get him out of here. Now! Take him somewhere and keep him there. He's insulted Sam Gundy, wiped out the pâté sandwiches, and he's monopolizing the press."

"Right."

"And find out where he got the tux jacket."

"Yes sir."

Half an hour later, Pete pulled the Porsche into Louisa's designated parking space and cut the ignition.

"Maybe this is all just a bad dream," Louisa said. "Maybe today never happened. I'm going to go to bed now, and maybe things will be better when I wake up."

Pete followed her to the door and stood patiently while she opened it. "It's not so bad, you know."

"Uh-huh."

"No one got hurt, and we got to go to a neat party."

"You *crashed* that neat party. And you insulted poor Sam Gundy."

"Hey, I even got dressed up. I wore my tux."

Louisa let her gaze travel the length of him. "What about the jeans and sneakers?"

"What about them?"

Louisa unlocked her door and stepped into the foyer. Pete followed. "Where do you think you're going?" she asked.

"I figured you'd want to offer me a drink or something."

"Nothing! I'm not going to offer you anything! And I don't want you in my house."

"How about coffee? Do I get a cup of coffee?"

"How about a knuckle sandwich? How'd you like that?"

He smiled and hooked his thumbs through his belt loops. "I suppose this means a good-night kiss is out of the question."

"Out!" She pointed stiff-armed to the door. "Out, out, out."

Pete came awake with an uneasy feeling in the pit of his stomach. He lay perfectly still, waiting for the confusion of sleep to leave him, wondering what had nudged him toward consciousness. He felt the cat shift at the foot of the bed, heard it growl low in its throat. Pete's eyes fastened on the VCR display across the room with the LED lights glowing red in the darkness. The lights went black for a moment, then reappeared, and Pete knew someone was silently moving around his bedroom. A body had passed between him and the LED lights. Reason told him to stay calm. Instinct told him to panic. Instinct won out. He sprang from the bed in one quick movement and hit the floor running, heading for the door. Halfway across the room he collided with the intruder, and they both went down in a heap on the floor.

Louisa sat at her kitchen table, elbows resting on the table, chin resting on her hands. She glumly looked at the clock on the wall. Three-fifteen. She couldn't sleep. Once again, it was all *his* fault. The fiend upstairs was keeping her awake. This time he was stomping around in her mind. She couldn't stop thinking about him. She sighed and slumped a little lower. She was in bad shape. Pete Streeter had looked good to her earlier. When he'd made the crack about the good-night kiss, she'd actually given it a second thought. She pushed away from the table and shuffled over to the refrigerator. She opened the door and stared at the bottles and jars for a while before deciding on orange juice. Hers was a normal reaction, she told herself. Streeter was gorgeous. Any healthy, sexually deprived woman would find Streeter attractive— unless she lived with him, of course. To live with Streeter was to hate him.

She drank her orange juice and padded back to the bedroom. She was about to crawl into bed when there was a loud thump overhead. It was followed by more thumping, then a crash that made her ceiling shake. She rolled her eyes. He was at it again. The man had no consideration. "Quiet!" she shouted. "Don't you know what time it is? It's three-fifteen in the morning!"

There was another ceiling-shaking crash, more thumping and scuffling sounds. "This is too much," Louisa muttered. "I absolutely am not going to tolerate this any longer."

She cinched her floor-length blue velour robe around herself with a vicious yank on the belt, stuffed her feet into her big furry slippers, and charged out of her bedroom. On the front porch she pounded on Streeter's door. "Open this door!" she demanded. She gave the door another shot with her fist, it swung open, and she stepped into the foyer. "Streeter, what the hell are you doing up there? I'm trying to get some sleep! I have to be at work early tomorrow!" Her only answer was more thrashing and grunting. She rolled her eyes. The man was exercising!

"Streeter!" Still no response. Big surprise, she thought. How could he possibly hear anything over the racket he was making. She flicked the light switch on, scooped her robe up into her hands, and climbed the stairs to his apartment. Standing in the dimly lit living room, she realized Pete was rolling around in his bedroom in the dark, and had a brief flash of panic that he might not be alone, that he might be in the throes of passion. She did more eye rolling and reminded herself that it didn't matter what the man was doing; the point being he was doing it too loud.

She held her ground in the middle of the living room and yelled in the direction of the bedroom. "Listen, Streeter, you macho crumb—"

A four-letter word carried out to her, and two

men tumbled through the bedroom door in a tangle of flailing arms and legs. They crashed into Louisa, taking her down with them, knocking the air out of her lungs. One of the men was clothed. One was naked. The naked one was Pete Streeter. Louisa didn't have time to ogle as the three of them rolled across the floor and down the stairs. They landed with a thud, smashing into a brass umbrella stand. The intruder scrambled to his feet and hustled out the door, down the steps, into a waiting car. Louisa and Pete lay dazed on the hardwood floor.

"So," Pete finally said, "couldn't sleep?"

"I'm afraid to ask what you were doing with that guy."

"What did it look like?"

"It looked like you were fighting."

Streeter stood. "That about sums it up."

Louisa was relieved. She was afraid it had been something kinky. She pulled herself to her feet, ran her tongue over her teeth to make sure none were missing, and willed her eyes to focus above Streeter's shoulders. It was hopeless. In her mind she was looking into his eyes, but in reality she was staring below the waist. "Jeez," Louisa said.

Pete's left eye was beginning to swell shut and he could taste blood in his mouth. He sighed. This was not a good time to be naked with Louisa Brannigan. "I'm not at my best," he told her.

She was still staring. She couldn't help herself. "Could have fooled me."

Pete lifted a trench coat from a wall peg and buttoned himself into it. "I think there's a compliment in there somewhere."

"What was this all about?"

"I don't know. I didn't get a chance to talk to the guy."

"This sort of thing happen to you a lot?"

"You mean rolling down the stairs naked with two other people?"

She shook her head. "You look terrible. You want me to drive you to the emergency room?"

"Not necessary. I'll be okay. I just need some ice."

"How about if I do my nurse thing and pour salt in your wounds?"

He grimaced. He was half afraid she meant it. "Sounds like fun, but I think I'll pass."

She touched his hand. "I'm serious. Are you going to be all right?"

"I'll be fine. In a half hour I'll have convinced myself I won." He turned her around and pushed her out the door. "I'm going to stay here until I hear your bolt slide across." And the next day he'd have better locks installed—and a security system.

Louisa crawled into bed with her robe still on and huddled under the covers. Now that she was alone, her teeth were chattering from fear and from the horror of seeing Pete Streeter cut and bruised. He was in trouble, she thought. Big trouble. She ordered herself to relax, to take deep breaths. The trembling stopped, but the panic remained, hollowing out her stomach, constricting her breathing. She wasn't sure if she was afraid for herself or for Streeter. Their lives suddenly seemed to be hopelessly entangled. And for all his annoying habits, she felt drawn to him. There was no denying it . . . the man had style. He was fascinating. He might even be likable under more favorable circumstances, although that was pushing it some.

The panic lifted and an equally potent but entirely different emotion fluttered in her stomach. She was smitten with Pete Streeter, she reluctantly admitted. Probably it wasn't so bizarre as it seemed, she told herself. After all, it was probably normal to feel a certain intimacy after tumbling down the stairs with a naked man. The memory brought a smile to her lips and another flutter in the pit of her stomach. She closed her eyes and reconstructed Streeter, vividly remembering every little detail . . . and one detail in particular that wasn't little at all.

At ten-thirty the following morning Louisa returned home. She slammed her front door with enough force to rattle windows, flung her briefcase halfway across the living room, and dropped her dress-for-success coat on the floor and kicked it. She marched into the kitchen and rummaged through her cabinet for a dish that was chipped. Then she took the chipped dish and threw it at the wall. She paused and took several deep breaths. Good. She was feeling much better. She was almost calm. Pretty soon she might even be rational. More deep breaths. A tear rolled down her cheek, and she quickly wiped it away, furious with herself that she'd allowed it to surface. She poured herself a cup of coffee, heated it in the microwave, and took it to the little cherrywood kitchen table. She had to think.

Ten minutes later she found herself knocking on Pete's front door.

He opened the door and squinted from behind a black eye. "I figured either you came home early or else there was a raging bull elephant loose in your apartment."

"We need to talk."

"Your place or mine?"

She thought about the pieces of broken crockery laying on her kitchen floor and decided she'd prefer he didn't know she'd been deranged. "Yours."

He moved slowly going up the stairs.

"How do you feel?" she asked.

"Like I've been run over by a tank."

The ground floor of the row house had been converted into a traditional apartment with living room, dining room, kitchen, and bedroom. The second floor, Louisa realized, was essentially two rooms—the bedroom, and a large room with the kitchen area to the rear. It had hardwood floors covered by Oriental carpets, big heavy furniture in muted tones, an odd assortment of tables, black-shaded brass lamps, and the largest large-screen TV she'd ever seen. One wall was devoted to bookshelves, their contents spilling over into a workstation that held a computer and laser printer.

Pete turned to her. "Is this going to be serious talking?"

"Yeah."

He led her to the kitchen table. "Did you get to drink the coffee you made?"

"How do you know I made coffee?"

"You heat coffee for one minute in the microwave. It comes through loud and clear."

She nodded. "Actually, I forgot to drink it. I was thinking."

He filled a mug and handed it to her.

She looked at it skeptically. It smelled like coffee, but she wasn't sure. "How do you get it this consistency?" she asked. "It looks like motor oil."

"The trick is to let it sit a few days."

She took a sip and sucked in her breath. "Holy cow."

"Too strong?"

"Don't you worry about it eating through the bottom of the mug?"

He pushed a cookie jar in her direction. "So what's your problem?"

"I've been fired." She took a cookie and nibbled on it. "Nolan called me into his office, asked a few questions about my relationship with you, and next thing, I'm told my services are no longer needed."

"Has to make you wonder."

"I thought you might be able to shed some light on my sudden termination."

"No advance warning?"

"None." She watched him expectantly. If he said 'bummer,' she'd hit him.

Pete felt the anger knot in his stomach. They were going too far. He could understand trying to cover dirty laundry, but this went way beyond anything he'd anticipated. Not that violence and intimidation were unprecedented in American political history. It was that he'd never been the direct recipient, and now the harassment was spreading to people associated with him.

He leaned back in his chair and debated how much he should tell her. He didn't know her very well. Instinct told him she was too goofy to be devious, but it wouldn't hurt to be careful. He linked his hands behind his head while he thought for a moment. "A couple weeks ago a newspaper article caught my attention. It was just one of those little filler things . . . boy bites dog stuff. It was about a pig that was running around loose in the halls of Congress. This probably sounds dumb, but I kept wondering about that pig. I kept wondering what happened to him."

Louisa grimaced. "You must have a lot of time on your hands."

He leaned forward. "You know anything about this pig?"

"Sure. The pig was supposed to be sent to Amsterdam as part of a goodwill animal husbandry exchange program. The program was sponsored by Stu Maislin. This particular pig had been bred in Maislin's home state and genetically altered to have an incredibly low fat ratio. The pig was brought to Maislin's office for publicity pictures. After the pictures were taken, the pig was scheduled to fly out of Dulles, but it got sick. My understanding is that everyone was scurrying around, trying to figure out what to do with a sick two-hundred-pound pig, and the pig mysteriously disappeared."

"How could it have disappeared? It was in the Hart Building, for crying out loud."

Louisa shrugged. "It was a Saturday. There weren't many people around."

"There were guards."

"Maybe one of the guards took it home and barbecued it."

"I thought of that," he said. "I've talked to all of the guards working that day. No one would admit to seeing it. I posted a reward for news of the pig. I made it easy for the informant to remain anonymous."

She paused and stared at him with her cookie midway to her mouth. "Why on earth would you go to all that trouble?"

"It didn't add up to me. My curiosity was aroused." That plus the fact that he was researching Maislin for his new screenplay and had heard some odd rumors about drug use and mob influence.

Louisa surveyed the man sitting across from her. He looked to be in his late thirties. He obviously had a lot of money and a certain

amount of fame, but he had few pretentions. He
didn't drop names, didn't wear flashy clothes,
didn't buy designer cookies. He made the world's
worst coffee, he wondered about pigs in Congress, and he looked great naked. She didn't
have a clue about his honesty, and she suspected his morals were shaky. "You seem sort of
obsessed by this filler."

"I've written screenplays about the black mar-
ket arms network, about Wall Street scandals,
about open-air drug dealers," Pete said. "I've
interviewed murderers, madmen, child molest-
ers. I've never before run into the kind of intimidation I'm getting on this pig thing. I started
receiving threatening phone calls after I posted
the first ad. I ran an ad in the paper, and
someone tried to wreck my car. I've had my
apartment broken into, and I've been attacked
in bed. Now you've been fired."

"Are you telling me I was fired because of a
pig?"

He shrugged. "Can you come up with any
better reasons?"

It sounded pretty farfetched. She was known
for being gullible, but this strained the limits of
credulity. And she definitely didn't trust Pete.
He looked like a man who would tell a woman
anything. If he'd told her he was a drug runner,
a known felon, a serial bank robber, she'd have
believed him in an instant. The pig story was
harder to swallow. On the other hand, even a
creative person like a writer would have a hard
time coming up with something that bizarre on

such short notice. And the bottom line was that it didn't matter if she believed him or not—she didn't have anything else. She recalled the shoving match between Maislin and Bishop outside the Hart Building and wondered if it was significant. "Okay, I'll go with it for a while," she said. "What have you found out about the pig that I don't already know?"

"Not much. I need someone on the inside. Someone like you. You want to join forces?"

"I'm not on the inside anymore. Security reclaimed my badge."

"You still know people."

It was true. She knew a lot of people, and she'd had something similar in mind when she'd stormed up the stairs. She intended to get to the bottom of this. Being summarily dismissed by Nolan would put a black mark on her résumé that would be hard to erase. She didn't intend to be gracious about it. She also didn't intend to let Pete get the upper hand in their partnership. She'd seen his type before. He was a bulldozer. If she wasn't careful, he'd be ordering her around, sending her off to chase down pigs. And even worse, if she wasn't *very* careful, she'd find herself in his bed and wondering how she got there. She'd play it cool. Not look too anxious. "I'll have to think about it."

"Honey, you're unemployed. What have you got to lose?"

It was a question that brought her eyebrows halfway up to her forehead.

Pete pushed back from the table. "Don't look

so alarmed. I happen to know you already lost that."

So much for cool, she thought. It was hard to be cool with a man who'd spent the last three weeks listening to her telephone conversations. "Okay, I'll throw in with you. Just don't get any wrong ideas."

He was standing behind her, thinking she'd be on her feet and running down the stairs if he told her about some of his ideas. He bent forward and whispered in her ear. "We are about to embark on an undercover operation—a pig hunt that could have a significant impact on national security and international relations. We have to trust each other, Lou. We have to work as a team. We have to . . . share." He kissed her just below her ear and again at the nape of her neck.

She swiveled in her chair, coming nose-to-nose with him. She narrowed her eyes and poked a forefinger at his chest. "Back off."

"I can't," he said, placing both hands on the table, trapping her. "I've developed an intense physical attraction to you."

"Good grief." It was a relief to know the attraction was reciprocal. It was disconcerting to have it put so bluntly.

A smile curved the corners of his mouth when he spoke. "I can tell you're excited about this newfound intimacy."

Terrified would be closer to the truth, she thought. An attraction was one thing, acting on that attraction was something entirely different.

"I'm not going to have to spend all my time in a groping war with you, am I?"

"Not for the next few days. I'm going to let my body heal before I do any serious groping." Probably a lie, he thought, but it wouldn't hurt to throw her off guard. He pushed away and grabbed his jacket from the elaborate oak coatrack at the top of the stairs. "Come on. Let's do some detecting. Let's check up on this Maislin dude. Let's see if he lives with piggies."

"Suppose we find Maislin has the pig. What does that prove?"

Pete shrugged. "I don't know. It's a place to start. I figure we'll just keep poking around, picking up stray pieces, and then at some point maybe the pieces will start to come together. Besides, even if Maislin doesn't have the pig, I'd still like to see his house."

Three

Louisa ran her finger down the congressional directory on her lap. "Maislin," she said. "Here it is . . . he lives in Potomac."

Pete turned off Connecticut, heading west to Wisconsin. He opened the sunroof, punched a Stones tape into the tape deck, and gave the console and floor mats a quick look to see if he'd left any loose cigarettes lying around. If he found one, he'd have an obligation to smoke it, he told himself. After all, it'd be just one, and then it wouldn't be there to tempt him in the future. He searched through the map pocket on the driver's side door and looked in the glove compartment. No cigarettes. Not even a butt. He sighed and slumped a little in his seat. "You smoke?" he asked Louisa.

"No."

"You drink?"

"A little wine once in a while."

"How about gambling . . . you go to the track? You buy lottery tickets?"

"No."

"So what are your secret vices?" He knew it wasn't sex. Her life was a sexual wasteland. "What do you do for fun?" he asked her. "You a chocolate binger? You have a fetish for kitchen appliances?"

"Being Nolan's press secretary has been pretty consuming. I guess I haven't done much else. Haven't really wanted to." She replaced the congressional directory with a map of Montgomery County and traced down Maislin's street. "I know this section of Potomac. The lots are all about two acres and the houses are so big, there's barely any lawn. Maislin isn't hurting for money."

Pete knew more than that. Maislin had started out with ball bearings. They went into everything from roller skates to rocket launchers. Over the years Maislin had diversified to nuts and bolts, electronic circuit boards, high-tech fuses, and a scattering of related industries. After his appointment to Congress, he'd dumped legal title into trusts and holding companies, so he couldn't be accused of conflicting interests. That didn't mean he didn't have any.

Pete turned north onto River Road. It was two lanes and filled with lights, but it was the most direct route to Potomac. He folded a stick of gum into his mouth and offered one to Louisa. "I'm much better at starting bad habits than stopping them," he said.

"Think you'll make it?"

"If I live long enough."

He drove by the outskirts of Glen Echo and passed under the beltway at Cabin John. The countryside was beginning to open up. The wealth was obvious. Houses were large. Grounds were manicured. "You're the navigator from here on," he said to Louisa.

"Take the next left."

The road led them into a subdivision of tract mansions. After half a mile Louisa pointed to a million-dollar version of a French country house. "There." A gray Mercedes was parked in the circular drive. "Now what?"

"I don't know," Pete said. "I guess I was hoping there'd be pigs on his front lawn." The street wasn't heavily traveled, so Pete stared at the house for a while. No one went in or out. No one peeked from behind drawn curtains. No pigs could be heard squealing in the distance. "I suppose one or both of us should try to get into the house," he finally said.

As far as Louisa was concerned he might as well have suggested they fly to the moon. "Forget it. Not me. No way."

He made chicken noises and flapped his arms. "No."

"You could be the Avon Lady."

"Get serious," Louisa said. "I'm not going in there."

"Does Maislin's wife know you?"

"I don't think so. They travel in higher circles."

Pete pulled the Porsche into the drive and parked next to the Mercedes.

Louisa had her hand braced against the dash. "I'm not getting out."

"Sure you are. We're a team. Wither thou goest."

"No!"

"C'mon, be a good girl and do this for Uncle Pete. I'll buy you an ice-cream cone."

"You're certifiable."

"Yeah, but I'm also lovable," he said. He took a pair of aviator sunglasses from the console and put them on. "Sexy, huh?"

She reluctantly followed him up the steps and lagged behind when he rang the bell. She couldn't imagine what he was going to say when the door opened. She was sure it would be something outrageous. After all, he was from California. He was involved in movies. He had a ponytail. "Listen," she said, "I was born and raised in Chevy Chase, Maryland. I'm not good at breaking and entering."

"This isn't going to be breaking and entering. This is going to be lying and entering."

"If I get arrested, my mother will have a heart attack."

"You're not going to get arrested. The worst that can happen is maybe this will be a little embarrassing."

"Oh Lord," she wailed. "I *hate* being embarrassed!" She wheeled around and headed for the car, but he grabbed her by the back of her jacket and pulled her to him. He firmly tucked her under his arm and rang the bell.

"Behave yourself," he said. "All you have to do is follow me around and look adoring. I'll do the talking."

The Maislin's front door cracked open, and a teenager peered out. Louisa guessed the girl to be fourteen or fifteen. She had a pouty cherub face, and she was wearing enough eye makeup to send the cosmetic company's stock up two points. Her hair was dyed raspberry, pulled into a ponytail that sprouted high on the right side of her head. She was wearing long johns, army combat boots, and an oversized black sweatshirt with a stretched-out neck that drooped over one shoulder.

"Uh-huh?" the teenager said.

Pete flashed her his Hollywood smile. "Hi. I'm Pete Streeter, and this is my associate." He made a vague hand gesture in Louisa's direction, but his eyes never strayed from the young woman in front of him. "I'm scouting movie locations—"

"Ommigod. Ommigod," the girl said. "Pete Streeter! I saw you on MTV. You were on the cover of *Premiere*. Ommigod, this is so awesome."

He turned the wattage up on the smile. "I'm in Washington doing a new screenplay, and like I said, I've been out scouting locations. I wonder if we could come in for a minute?"

"Ommigod, you want to use this house in a

movie? I can't believe it. That would be like so excellent."

"There might even be a small part in it for you," Pete said.

Louisa made a gagging sound behind him.

"What's wrong with her?" the girl asked. "Why is she making those megagross sounds?"

"She's pregnant," Pete told her. "She has morning sickness all day long. It's really pretty disgusting. Try to ignore her."

Louisa kicked him in the back of the leg, and he took a blind swipe at her, catching her on the shoulder, knocking her off balance.

"Radical," the teenager said. "Very alpha."

Pete moved toward the back of the house. "You don't mind if I look around, do you?" He walked through the dining room, into the kitchen. "What's your name?"

"Amy Maislin."

"Why aren't you in school?"

"It's the end of the grading period. It's a teacher work day, and we get the day off. I was supposed to go to the mall, but the Mercedes is sick."

"Bummer," Pete said. He looked out the French doors. The yard was small for the size of the house. There was a flagstone patio with white wrought-iron furniture that looked cold and uninviting. Beyond the patio was a pool, protectively covered in blue vinyl. Some fancy shrubbery delineated the end of the property. He didn't see any pigs.

"So what do you think?" Amy asked. "You think this will do?"

He turned from the doors and scanned the kitchen. It didn't look any more promising than the yard—no bags of pig chow sitting around. "You have any pets?"

"A dog. He's downstairs in the work-out room with my mom. She's into this physical stuff."

"That's it? A dog?"

Amy looked worried. "Is that bad? Did you want a house with cats or something? I could get a cat."

"Actually, I was looking for a house with a pig," Pete said.

"Far out," Amy said. "I could dig a house with a pig, but I don't know any. How about a rabbit? My friend, Christy, has a rabbit. I could borrow it and maybe we could shave it and tie down its ears. And then you could like do special effects."

"I'll keep it in mind," Pete said. "Thanks for showing me the house."

"Gnarly," she said. "And I think your hair is bitchin'."

Pete saw Louisa's eyes widen. "It's a compliment," he told her, guiding her out the front door.

"I know that. We say that to each other on Capitol Hill all the time."

He smiled at her and got a smile in return.

"Now what?" Louisa asked, settling herself into the Porsche.

"I don't know. This was our one lead. I'm

usually much more clever than this," he told her. "The problem is I have these cravings . . ."

"Nicotine withdrawal?"

"Yeah, that too."

"Maybe lunch would help."

He found his way back to River Road and headed for the district. Lunch wasn't a bad idea, he thought. Someplace dark and cozy. Someplace where they could get to know each other better: Favorite color, siblings, sexual preferences. And it should be close to home in case they got carried away. He didn't think it would take much to get him carried away. He was already halfway there. "I know a place on Connecticut," he said.

"Can you wait that long?"

"If I have to."

Louisa was apprehensive when she saw his choice. She balked at the door. "This is very nice, but I had something different in mind."

"What did you have in mind?"

No sense trying to be tactful, she thought. There really was no easy way to put it. "Something cheap," she said. "I'm unemployed."

"My treat."

"Nice, but no thanks. There's a sandwich shop on the next block . . ."

Pete slung his arm around her shoulder. He was becoming very fond of her. She was a good sport. She'd only whined a little on the way back to town, and he respected her honesty. There was nothing wrong with admitting you didn't have any money. He figured since she was so honest, she'd appreciate him being up-front with her. "I've been to that sandwich shop. It's always busy, and it has bright lights and lots of noise." He leaned into her and nuzzled the nape of her neck. "This restaurant, on the other hand, has tiny tables and long tablecloths and is dark enough for—"

"This is *not* a date. And I don't . . . do whatever in public."

"Oh, man, give me a break, Lou. I quit smoking. Look at me, I'm in sensory deprivation. I'm going on frustration overload. I have appetites. I have needs."

She turned on her heel and headed out the door. "You're in big trouble if those needs can't be satisfied with a sandwich."

He followed her down Connecticut. "You're a tough woman, you know that? Where's your compassion? Where's your sense of charity?"

Louisa rolled her eyes. "Is that what you want? You want me to take pity on you?"

"Yeah."

She looked at him in amazement.

"It's a start," he said, grinning.

She opened the door to the sandwich shop and motioned him in. "You must really be desperate."

"I think I'm in love."

Her eyebrows raised. "Maybe I should buy you some cigarettes."

"I bet you're in love too," he said.

"You're an odious person. You steal, you lie,

you're insensitive, inconsiderate, you're a womanizer, and you make horrible coffee."

"I could learn how to make better coffee."

Louisa slid into a booth and looked at the menu. "I'll have the number three club," she told the waitress.

"Steak sandwich," Pete said. He slouched into a corner and stretched his legs the length of the seat. "I'll concede to being all of those awful things, if you'll agree to list my good qualities."

Louisa stared at him. "Good qualities. This is going to be tough."

His smile broadened.

He was smug, she thought. Add that to insensitive and inconsiderate. She searched her mind for good qualities. She came up empty. A small frown developed between her eyebrows. Ridiculous as it seemed, she liked him. And it wasn't just sexual, although the sexual attraction was frighteningly strong. He was fun, and he was comfortable. He was impossible to insult. She wouldn't exactly call it a good quality, but it was a nice change of pace after years of Capitol Hill diplomacy. And she liked the way he was honest about lying.

"Well?" he asked.

"I'm thinking."

"Jeez. It's taking *this* long to come up with one good quality?"

"Maybe I just don't know you well enough."

"Okay, I'll help you out. I happen to have a wonderful sense of humor. I pay almost all my parking tickets. I like small animals and big children. I hardly ever cuss at old people. I've never shot anyone on the freeway. I gave a dollar to a bum yesterday."

"This is very impressive."

"Damn right. I could go on, but I'm getting embarrassed."

"I bet you're incredibly romantic too."

"Do bears do it in the woods?"

"I'm overwhelmed."

In truth, he worked very hard to keep his romantic inclinations under control. He allowed only a thin thread of romanticism to work its way into his screenplays, and he kept a tight lid on it in his everyday life. He felt screenplays grew maudlin with a surfeit of romance, and men became vulnerable. He didn't count candy and flowers and elegant restaurants as being high on the romance scale—they were clichés and more often than not impersonal gestures. That didn't mean he wasn't above using them to achieve a desired result. He wasn't a stupid man, and he knew women expected the conventional niceties. But in his heart, he felt romance should be a very private matter.

"Maybe we should get back to serious talk," Louisa said. "I don't want to become so carried away with your good qualities that I lose perspective. It wouldn't do to spend the afternoon dallying around when there are pigs to be found."

Pete was becoming less interested in pigs by the minute. He was much more interested in the fact that Louisa Brannigan had flawless milk-white skin, a snippy little nose, a short fuse, and a large chunk of stubborn. He liked the way her eyes lit up when she smiled, and the way her nose wrinkled when she was mad. He couldn't imagine her towing the line as a congressional press secretary. He thought it must have been a strain on a personality that he suspected leaned toward the volatile.

Her voice sobered. "This is important to me. I've had my car trashed, I've been rolled down a flight of stairs in the middle of the night, and I've lost my job. I want to know why."

"You want to get revenge?"

"Nothing that dramatic. I just want to stay clean. I don't know the extent of Nolan's involvement. I don't want to turn out to be an unwitting accomplice to something ugly." And while she didn't want to articulate it to Pete, other emotions were gnawing at her. The disappointment in Nolan was almost crushing. She'd believed in him, trusted him to do the right thing, had faith in his abilities. She'd put herself on the line for him, touting his potential with next-to-religious fervor. Even if he wasn't directly involved in whatever was rotten, he'd dismissed her too easily. Her sense of betrayal was strong. She was an idealist, she realized. She suspected it was a term synonymous with young and foolish, but she was stuck with it all the same. Her moral and political indignation was aroused.

Pete's reasons for pursuing the pig cover-up had little to do with moral or political indignation. Simple curiosity had turned to certain knowledge that he'd stumbled onto a scandal of some sort. It was grist for his creative mill. It was a potential screenplay. It had also piqued his male ego. He had inadvertently opened up a can of worms, and the folks holding the can had misjudged him. He wasn't the sort of person who yielded to pressure. He resented being threatened, and he was furious he'd been attacked in his sleep. The most serious mistake made was in firing Louisa. He hated to admit it, but he felt intensely protective of her. Not that she seemed to need protection—if she needed anything, it was restraint, Pete thought. If left to her own devices, she'd probably end up in a homicide lineup for death by broom handle.

"Okay," Pete said, "let's see what we have here. We know Maislin was the pig shipper. We know someone doesn't want questions asked about the little porker. And we know Nolan Bishop fired you because of your association with me. From this overwhelmingly damning evidence we're concluding that both Maislin and Bishop are involved in something nasty."

"Doesn't sound incredibly conclusive, does it?"

He made a noncommittal shrug. "What do Maislin and Nolan Bishop have in common?"

"They both belong to the same party."

"What else?"

Louisa thought about it. They were from different states. Maislin was from Pennsylvania. Nolan was from Maryland. Both lived in Potomac when Congress was in session. Maislin was a blue-color success story. Nolan was Harvard law. On the surface they didn't have much in common, but both men were extremely ambitious. Both cared a great deal about public opinion.

"Are they buddies?"

"Not that I know of. Maislin's been around longer. Carries a lot more clout. He travels with the Big Boys."

"You ever have to sit on any bad publicity for Nolan?"

"Nope."

"Any sexual indiscretions?"

"Nothing past the leering stage since I've been with him."

Conversation momentarily stopped while the food was served.

"How about Maislin?" Pete asked.

Louisa picked at her sandwich, eating the bacon first. "I don't know much about Maislin. As far as I know he keeps himself clean. He's on some powerful committees, his constituents are fond of him, and he's not too bright."

"There has to be more of a connection," Pete said.

"After lunch I'll go back to my office and clean out my desk. I'll get a profile on Maislin while I'm there."

It was dark when Louisa staggered up the porch stairs, carrying a large cardboard box filled with personal belongings, daily calenders, her Rolodex, and as much information as she'd been able to gather on both Maislin and Nolan Bishop. She fumbled in her purse for the key and let herself into the empty apartment. She slid the bolt on the lock, turned the light on with her elbow, and collapsed into an overstuffed chair with the box on her lap. Her heart stopped beating at the sound of a key turning in her lock, and she let out a bloodcurdling scream when the door opened. It was Pete. She closed her eyes, clapped her hand to her chest, and sunk deeper into the chair. "Good Lord."

"Did I scare you?"

"Hell no. I always scream like that when people come into my apartment." She looked up at him. "How did you do that? How did you unlock my door?"

"I have a key. I own this place."

"Wonderful. That makes me feel so much safer. Not only do I have to worry about the pig people; now I have to worry about my sneaky landlord."

He took the box and tucked it under his arm. "Good thing I have a healthy ego. You're not the most supportive girlfriend I've ever had."

"I'm not your girlfriend."

He pulled her to her feet and pushed her toward the door. "Whatever."

"Where are we going?"

"My place. We'll brainstorm over dinner."

She followed him up the stairs to the kitchen

area, and gaped at the big orange cat sprawled across the butcher-block table. It had one ear half chewed off and a pronounced kink in its tail. "You have a cat on your table," Louisa said.

"Yeah. That's Spike."

Spike opened one eye and looked at Louisa. The eye was yellow and unblinking. It stared at Louisa for thirty seconds and closed, leaving Louisa with the impression she'd been less than interesting.

Pete set the cardboard box next to the sleeping cat. "Ten years ago Spike sort of adopted me, and we've been together ever since." He scratched the cat's head, but the cat didn't move. "He's very demonstrative," Pete said.

"I can see that."

Pete took a bottle of wine from the refrigerator, filled a crystal wineglass half full, and handed the glass to Louisa. "Were you able to get much on Maislin?"

She sipped her wine. "The usual whitewashed press release."

Pete slid three steaks under the broiler and threw two potatoes into the microwave. He accepted a blue folder from Louisa, flipped it open, and began reading. "I can't see anything in here to help us," he finally said. He scooped Spike off the table and replaced him with a tossed salad he took from the refrigerator. Spike dangled bonelessly from the crook of Pete's arm. He slowly opened his eyes, yawned, and yowled. Pete speared one of the steaks from the broiler, flopped it onto a plate, and set cat and steak on the floor.

Louisa couldn't keep the astonishment from her voice. "You're giving him an entire steak?"

"Hey, this guy's a stud. He has to keep his strength up."

"Is that good for him? I mean, shouldn't he be eating cat food? You know, a balanced cat diet?"

Pete put a potato and a steak on a plate for Louisa. "We don't eat steak every night. Sometimes we eat fish. Sometimes we order out for pizza. His favorite is hamburger with a lot of fried onions. We eat that a lot."

Tell me about it, Louisa thought. Everything in her apartment smelled like Pete's fried onions. The odor had permeated her wallpaper. His apartment, she noticed, had no such problem. His apartment smelled fresh and clean, slightly of coffee. She glanced at the vent over the stove. It was busy sucking away the broiler smoke, no doubt sending it directly down to her kitchen.

He put a container of sour cream on the table and topped her wine. "How about Maislin's staff? Do we have any information on them?"

Louisa pulled another folder from the cardboard box. She gave the folder to Pete and attacked her steak.

Pete read while he ate, but he didn't find anything useful.

"That was great," Louisa said. She looked at her wineglass and wondered how it had gotten empty.

Pete took a quart of chocolate ice cream from the freezer and set it in the middle of the table. He gave Louisa a sterling silver iced-tea spoon and kept one for himself. "Let's go over this again," he said, digging into the ice cream. "Why is everyone so touchy about this pig?"

Louisa took a spoonful of ice cream and let it melt on her tongue. It was smooth and rich. It was the brand she couldn't afford, the one that clogged arteries with butterfat. Already, she could feel her thighs expanding. She took another spoonful, closed her eyes, and murmured approval. "This is wonnnnderful ice cream," she said, her eyes slightly glazed.

Pete stared at her. She was practically orgasmic. "Are you okay?" he asked.

"Couldn't be better. I lovvvvve ice cream." She had a large mound of ice cream on her spoon. She aimed it at her mouth, but it fell onto the table. "Oops," she said. "I think it's the wine. It sneaked up on me."

Pete smiled. She was snockered! "You're not much of a drinker, are you?"

"Am I acting silly?"

"Not yet."

"I tend to get uninhibited when I drink," she said.

"Oh boy."

"And then I get tired. Wine always makes me tired."

"How long would you say we've got between uninhibited and tired?"

"Not long. Minutes, actually."

"Is there anything you'd especially like to do while you're in the uninhibited stage?"

"Eat more ice cream."

He spooned ice cream into her. "Anything else?"

"We could talk. There are some things I should say to you."

"You really know how to bust loose when you're uninhibited, don't you?"

She smiled at him. "I have my moments."

"Is this one of them?"

Louisa waved her iced-tea spoon. "I was a late bloomer."

He crossed his arms on the table and leaned forward. He had a feeling this was going to be interesting.

"In fact, I didn't bloom at all until I was in college. And even then . . ." She sighed and dabbled in the ice cream carton. "I had this silly idea that I should be in love before I . . . you know."

"It's not a silly idea."

They both paused, each surprised he'd said such a thing.

"Do you make love to women you don't love?" she asked.

"Only if it's an emergency."

She made an effort to focus her eyes on him. "That's not a serious answer."

He reached across the table and took her hand. He turned it palm up and kissed the soft center. "I don't think either of us would like the serious answer."

Heat curled into her stomach and radiated outward at the touch of his lips on her flesh. "Have you ever been in love?"

It was a complicated question. Certainly, there'd been women about whom he'd felt deeply. And there's been a few voluptuous females early on who'd turned him inside out and left him flopping around like a beached flounder, struggling to survive. But he couldn't honestly say he'd ever been in love. Lately, he'd begun to wonder if he was capable of loving someone. "No," he told her. "I've never been in love."

"Me, either," she said, yawning. "I thought I was once, but it was just wishful thinking." She rested her head on the table and fell asleep.

Pete stared at her. He'd never seen anyone nod off on a glass and a half of wine before. He scooped her up and carried her to the couch. She was dressed in a soft pink suit, complete with tinted stockings and heels. He didn't know what to do with her. He had a strong temptation to loosen her clothes in the interest of comfort, but he resisted. She'd probably get the wrong idea and think he'd done it just to fondle her. She'd probably be right. He covered her with a quilt and went about the job of cleaning the kitchen. When he was done, he sat across from her on the coffee table and watched her sleep. She looked like a little girl, he thought. Her cheeks were flushed, her mouth soft and pouty, black lashes curved against her fine translucent skin. Her hair curled around her face in casual disarray. His throat felt tight and his heart ached with an emotion he couldn't identify. The ache in his groin was less confusing. He knew what was causing that. And he knew it was a lost cause.

Four

Louisa awakened to the aroma of bacon frying and the unpleasant sensation of having a crushing weight on her chest. The weight turned out to be Spike. He opened his yellow cat eyes and stared at her for several seconds before his lids dropped closed. Louisa shifted under him, and he growled low in his throat. Two masculine hands reached over Louisa's head and lifted the cat off her.

"Morning," Pete said.

Louisa tilted her head back to see him. "What happened?"

"You had a glass and a half of wine and fell asleep."

She took a fast survey of her condition. She was on his couch, fully clothed, under a quilt. "Have I slept here all night?"

"Yup."

She sighed. "I'm not very good at drinking."

She tugged at her skirt and swung her feet onto the floor, still swaddled in the quilt. "I make up for my alcohol intolerance with my temper. I inherited the belligerent gene."

He handed her a glass of freshly squeezed orange juice and a plate heaped with bacon and scrambled eggs.

"Thanks, Mom," she said.

He slouched in a chair across from her. He wasn't feeling especially maternal. He was feeling sexually frustrated and emotionally unstable. He'd spent the better part of the night staring at his bedroom ceiling, wondering what the hell he was doing with his life, wondering what it was about Louisa Brannigan that had him suddenly feeling dissatisfied and lonely. He could easily have awakened her and shuffled her off to her own apartment, but the simple truth was, he liked having her in his living room. Spike was a good friend, but he was small. He didn't fill the apartment the way Louisa did. Pete liked the way Louisa sighed and rustled when she slept. It was a comforting sound . . . like a crackling fire on a cold day, or rain against a windowpane.

She drank the juice and munched on a strip of bacon. "It feels strange not to have to rush off to work."

"What'll you do today?"

"Get my car fixed. Then I suppose I should start thinking about getting another job."

"I have a deal for you."

"Uh-oh."

"It's a good deal."

"I bet."

"I want to stick with this pig thing, but I'm running low on time. I have rewrites to do on a screenplay that's going into production next week."

She took a bite of egg. "And?"

"And I'll give you a month's free rent, if you'll hold off taking another job for a few days. I have my own file on Maislin. I'd like you to go through it and see if you can find a connection between him and Nolan Bishop. Then I'd like you to go to the *Post* building on L Street and read back issues on either side of the pig story."

The offer appealed to Louisa. The detecting part sounded like fun, and she couldn't turn her nose up at a month's free rent. Her savings account was going to be fast depleted without a job. "Okay, it's a deal. What am I searching for in the back issues?"

"I don't know. Keep an open mind."

She finished her breakfast and stood to leave, groaning when she looked down at her rumpled suit. "I'll take a fast shower and get right to work."

It was almost noon when Louisa finished reading Pete's file on Stuart Maislin. Spike was back to sleeping on the kitchen table, amidst the piles of news clippings and handwritten notes. Pete was slouched in a padded office chair, staring at the computer screen. He leaned forward and began typing. The soft click of computer keys carried across the room. Louisa crossed her arms on the table in front of her and watched him, thinking writing was a very quiet, very solitary profession. She'd expected the creative process to be more flamboyant, but Pete Streeter went about his rewrites in an orderly businesslike fashion. There was no hair pulling, no ranting, no empty whiskey glasses littering the work area, or balled-up, discarded sheets of paper spread across the floor. Sometimes his lips moved, but the sounds he made, if any, were soft, polite murmurings as he listened to the music of his written word. All this was very much at odds with the image she'd formed of him, and she found herself fascinated by this serious, introspective piece of his personality.

He finished his typing, stood, stretched, and looked over at Louisa. He raised his eyebrows in silent question.

"I'm done," Louisa said.

"Find anything?"

She tore the top two sheets off a yellow legal pad. "I have two pages of possible connections between Maislin and Bishop. Most of the connections are pretty obscure."

He moved behind her to pour himself a cup of coffee. "What looks good?"

"Actually, nothing looks good. It's possible that Nolan was just bowing to Maislin's wishes."

He looked at her over the rim of his coffee mug. "Is Nolan that much of a wimp?"

"He's that much of a politician. There's a lot of information here on Maislin's finances and business associates. Why?"

"I have an option on Judd King's book, *Power Players.* It suggests misconduct among some of the most influential members of Congress. The book is fiction, but supposedly King knew what he was talking about. He died three weeks after the book hit the stores. Brain tumor . . . just like Bill Casey. When I took the option on the book, I decided I needed to gather background information. Maislin's profile fits one of the men in King's book."

"How does the pig figure into all of this?" Louisa asked.

"I haven't a clue." He took a jar of chunky peanut butter and a jar of marshmallow fluff from the refrigerator. He set out a couple plates and a loaf of white bread.

Louisa slid a glance at the gooey marshmallow and peanut butter.

"Lunch," Pete said, smearing a thick coating of marshmallow onto a slice of bread. "This stuff is great. You can use it in everything." He added a slice of peanut butter bread and slapped the two halves together. He put the sandwich on a plate and set it front of Louisa. He poured her a glass of milk and gave her a banana.

Louisa bit down on her lower lip to keep from giggling. She felt as if she were back in grade school with her Snoopy lunch box and red plastic thermos. "Thank you," she said politely.

Pete gave a sandwich to Spike. Then he made

another for himself, settling into the chair across from Louisa.

"This is an interesting sandwich," Louisa said, struggling to keep her tongue from sticking to the roof of her mouth. She drank half a glass of milk and secretly felt her fillings to make sure they were intact.

"If I get bogged down in a script, peanut butter and marshmallow always picks me up. It's sort of inspirational."

Louisa continued to chew. It wasn't bad, but it needed chocolate. "So, did you eat this all the time when you were a kid?"

"Never. I was too tough to eat this sissy food. I ate burgers and beer and bologna sandwiches."

"I mean when you were seven."

He stared at her and for a moment his face lost its usual animation. His eyes seemed flat, his mouth tightened. Then the humor returned. "I was talking about seven."

"You're serious."

"Pretty much. My mother died when I was five. I was raised in an all-male household." He thought back to the ugly yellow clapboard house on Slant Street in Hellertown, Pennsylvania. It hadn't been a terrible childhood, but it hadn't been great, either. Mostly, it had been lonely and lacking the soft touches a woman brought to a home. By the time he was in first grade, his two older brothers had already quit school and gone to work in the steel mill with his dad. Back then, in his neighborhood, nobody cared about latch-key kids. Kids grew up fast on Slant Street, and it didn't matter that no one was home to supervise homework. The future was preordained: The men worked in the mill. They married young, and there were no subtleties to the mating process. It was a matter of personal pride and masculine obligation for every Slant Street male past the age of puberty to get his hand and whatever else he could manage under as many skirts as possible. When a girl got pregnant, she singled out her best prospect, they got married in full regalia at St. Stanislaus, had the reception in the firehouse, and settled into the tedium of premature old age.

And that would have been his future, Pete thought, but thanks to his good luck, none of the women who'd gone past his doorstep had gotten pregnant. And by the time he was eighteen, his reputation was so bad, his police record so lengthy with misdemeanors that he couldn't get a job in the mill. Take it to the limit. Never do anything halfway. He'd been a truly rotten kid. Even his own brothers, who'd been pretty bad in their times, couldn't touch him.

Louisa finished her sandwich and ate her banana. "You ever been married? You ever live with anyone?"

"Only Spike."

That explained it. She was beginning to understand the origin of some of his more annoying habits. He was severely lacking in female guidance. He didn't know any of the niceties of life. Dollars to doughnuts he left the toilet seat up. She put her dishes in the dishwasher and stacked the files in the cardboard box. "I'm off to the *Post.*"

"Be careful."

"Of what?"

"Mean dogs, dirty old men, drunk drivers . . ." He sighed with disgust at his own foolishness, grabbed hold of the front of her baggy University of Maryland sweatshirt, pulled her to him, and kissed her. She tasted like dessert. Life didn't get much better, Pete thought. This was the filet of existence. He opened his eyes and realized she was staring at him. "Something wrong?"

Her face had turned scarlet. She looked down at the sweatshirt still bunched in his hand. "You've accidentally unhooked the front closure to my bra."

His grin was lazy, his eyes soft with a mixture of sensuality and amusement. It had been no accident. He had one of the most talented thumbs in the country . . . maybe in the world. "Sorry," he said, releasing the shirt. "Guess I got carried away." He stuffed his hands into his pockets and rocked back on his heels. He was finally in love. No doubt about it.

Louisa buttoned her navy pea coat up to her throat as she left the *Post* building and walked west to the Farragut North Metro station. She would have been done with the papers a lot sooner if Pete hadn't kissed her after lunch, she thought. Her mind had been stuck on it all afternoon. The kiss had been warm and friendly with just a suggestion of passion. In fact, it had been almost playful. Just what you'd expect from a man who ate marshmallow goop for lunch. Still, it had surprised her. She'd been mentally prepared for a different sort of kiss . . . a much more aggressive sort. She'd been ready to firmly reject his advances, and it hadn't been necessary. She reluctantly admitted she was experiencing an emotion that felt a lot like disappointment. She took the escalator to the underground lobby, bought a fare card, and passed through an electronic gate, telling herself there was no reason to be depressed just because she didn't inspire flaming passion in the man. After all, she'd told him on several occasions how much she disliked him. And she'd warned him against groping. It was just that she didn't know what to make of the kiss, she told herself. It had been so . . . happy.

She was still thinking about the kiss when she knocked on his front door a half hour later. "Reporting in on the newspaper assignment, sir," she said when he opened the door, the theory being when discombobulated over a sexual attraction, resort to juvenile behavior.

He closed his front door behind her, unbuttoned her jacket, pulled her to him by her lapels, and lowered his mouth to hers. It was a hello, welcome-home kiss. It was an I-like-you kiss. It was pretty damn happy. It was grossly disappointing. All lips and no tongue and much too short. Louisa swayed a little when he stepped away from her. "Darn," she said.

"Something wrong?"

"You unhooked my bra again."

"Must be a faulty clasp."

She narrowed her eyes at him. "I don't trust you."

"Boy, Lou, that really hurts. Here I've been slaving over a hot stove all day, making a nutritious home-cooked meal for you, and I get nothing but insults."

Louisa sniffed the air. It smelled wonderful—like spaghetti sauce and garlic bread. She trudged up the stairs and crossed to the kitchen area. The table was set for two with a white linen tablecloth, wineglasses, and lavender candles. There was a daisy on her plate. It only had one petal left. Without thinking, she automatically played the game and plucked the remaining petal, silently chanting "he loves me." She looked up and their eyes met.

"It's true," he said.

She rolled her eyes.

"You don't believe me?"

"Not for an instant."

Smart woman, he thought. He could hardly believe it himself. He dropped spaghetti into a pot of boiling water, took two salads from the refrigerator and garlic bread from the oven. He filled the wineglasses with seltzer. "Did you find anything interesting in any of the papers?"

She hung her coat on the coatrack and took a seat at the table. "No. There was just that one little article about the pig. Nothing about Maislin. Nothing I could pick up about any of his related interests." She watched him work at the stove, and thought it was nice that he'd gone to some trouble for her. He'd bought a daisy and set the table with linen and crystal. She wasn't sure of his motives, but she appreciated the effort all the same. And she had to admit, she enjoyed the companionship. Her eyes drifted the length of him, and desire rushed through her in a scalding wave that caused her to squirm in her seat. She shook her head and muttered a warning to herself. The intensity of the attraction was inappropriate. She didn't take sex lightly, and he wasn't a man she'd choose for a serious relationship. It was a waste of perfectly good hormones, she thought. She'd waited all these years for her body to respond to a man, and wouldn't you know it would be to a wrong number like Pete Streeter. There was no justice in the world.

Pete noticed she was muttering again. He brought the hot food to the table and watched for a few seconds while she conversed with herself. She was a little crazy, he decided. A jillion women in the world, and he had to fall in love with one who was crazy. It figured.

She smacked herself on the forehead with the heel of her hand. "Unh!"

"Now what?"

"And another thing," she said. "I'm not going to sleep with you, so you can just forget it."

He grinned and passed her the spaghetti. She was crazy all right, but it was kind of cute. "Of course you'll sleep with me."

A look of astonishment popped onto her face, and her mouth fell open.

He sighed and forked spaghetti onto her plate. Probably he shouldn't have said that, he thought. Sometimes it didn't pay to be entirely honest with women. He helped himself to the spaghetti and realized she was still sitting there in dumbfounded apoplexy so he spooned sauce over both their plates and added grated cheese. He didn't know why she looked so disconcerted. It was obvious they were going to be lovers. It was just a matter of time. True, she didn't think he was all that great right now, but he was sure she'd come around.

Louisa snapped her mouth closed and stabbed her fork into her spaghetti. Of all the nerve! If she wasn't so hungry, she'd get up and walk right out of there, she told herself, but no sense turning her back on a good meal. She tapped her fork against her plate and narrowed her eyes. "How can you be so sure we'll end up in bed?"

How could he be sure? Every instinct he possessed told him so. Being next to her was like getting trapped in a force field of carnal electricity. Every molecule in his body hummed with desire. And when he kissed her, he could feel her need for him. It was there. He was sure of it. Did she want to hear any of that? Probably not. He shrugged his shoulders and took a piece of warm bread. "I like to think positive."

Another whack on her forehead. "Unh!"

"I guess that means I said the wrong thing again."

"You have much success with women?"

"Well, I don't like to brag . . ."

Louisa held her hand up. "Stop. Forget I asked." It was a dumb question, anyway, she thought. Women probably threw themselves in front of his car for five minutes of attention. Probably, he had so many women following him around that he had to beat them off with a stick. Of course, that was because they didn't know about his laundry habits. "Maybe we should change the subject. Maybe we should get back to the pig problem."

"I'd like to take a look at the guy who delivered the pig. His name's Bucky Dunowski. He works at the pig farm as a security guard, and he lives a few miles south of the facility, just over the state line."

"You think he became attached to Miss Piggy and took her home?"

"Anything's possible. The pig farm is about an hour's drive from here . . . maybe a little longer. How about if we go to Pennsylvania tonight and check out ol' Bucky."

"Tonight?"

"Sure. It's perfect. We can sulk around in the dark, looking for pigs. No one will ever see us." He didn't really think he'd find a pig in Bucky's backyard, but skulking around in the dark with Louisa sounded like a good idea.

"No! Definitely not. It was bad enough lying to Amy Maislin. I am *not* going to Pennsylvania with you. And I am absolutely, positively not going to skulk."

Two hours later, Louisa slouched low in the Porsche as she looked for house numbers painted on mailboxes. They were in a mixed neighborhood of small, not especially well-kept bungalows and larger, newer homes. The houses were set on heavily treed lots, frequently separated by patches of woods. The street was dark and windy. Louisa shook her head in disbelief. Against her better judgment she was about to spy on Bucky Dunowski. Her mouth tightened into a grimace as she glanced over at Pete. His profile was outlined in moonlight, all mysterious shadows and hard, masculine planes. He was obscenely handsome and hopelessly well adjusted. He also had brass doodles and didn't know the meaning of the word no. Not the sort of man she wanted to become romantically involved with, she reminded herself for the umpteenth time. Unfortunately, that was an intellectual decision and had little bearing on her emotions. The truth was, Pete Streeter was looking better with each passing second. It was one of those miracles of nature—romantic dementia. And it occurred whenever she was within arm's reach of Streeter. His laundry habits were seeming trivial. His inability to find his own parking space was becoming endearing. The fit of his jeans overshadowed all else. She rested her forehead against the side window and sighed.

"Something wrong?"

"Only everything."

He patted her knee. "Good to know you're not one of those sickening optimists."

She noticed his hand was lingering on her leg. She should call his attention to it, she thought, but she wasn't sure she wanted him to remove it. His hand was warm and reassuring, and it was sending pleasurable sensations to other parts of her body. It had been a long time since she'd enjoyed those kinds of sensations. Now that she gave it serious thought, maybe she'd *never* experienced them. Certainly the feelings were beyond her memory. They rolled past two mailboxes before Louisa realized one of them must have been Bucky's. "Hold up," she said. "I think we just missed it."

Pete pulled onto the shoulder a few yards down the road. "This is a good place to park. It's dark and fairly secluded." He slid his arm across the back of her seat. "We don't want to park where we can be seen," he said, trailing his hand over her shoulder, down her coat sleeve. He felt like Goldilocks, settling in to eat Little Bear's bowl of porridge. After all that previous sampling, he'd finally found a woman who was just right. The knowledge was more intuitive, more emotional than rational, but he'd always trusted his instincts, and he saw no reason not to trust them now.

He saw that she was very still, not moving from his touch. She was making decisions, he thought. She was trying to come to terms with her own feelings. He hoped she decided on positive action, because he was going on frustration overload. "You know, maybe we were hasty about this pig business. Maybe it's not such a good idea to go chasing around at night," he said. Maybe it would be better to stay here and take our clothes off, he thought. Disrobing in a Porsche wasn't his idea of the perfect prelude to lovemaking, but he was willing to sacrifice comfort for the good of the cause. Besides, there was something to be said for spontaneity, right? And there was something to be said for sanity, and the fact that he was going to lose his if the cause didn't get served soon.

He tentatively caressed a silky tendril of her hair, and the contact sent affection surging through him. The affection tempered lust and provoked an attack of conscience. He knew he was rushing things. They'd only known each other for a few days, and she was still laboring under the delusion that she didn't like him. Encouraging her to take her clothes off probably wasn't a good idea. He didn't want to be accused of being pushy and of only having one thing on his mind . . . especially if it was true. His fingertip followed the curve of her ear down to the line of her jaw, and the contact sent another shot of desire pounding into his groin. He was engaging in self-indulgent torture, he thought. He'd be better off not to touch her at all, but he was incapable of exercising that much self-control. Nothing short of cutting off his hands would keep them from reaching out for Louisa. He skimmed his thumb over the pulse point, and his fingers curled around the nape of her neck, stroking, and unconsciously seducing.

He had wonderful hands, Louisa concluded, strong and sensual. She watched the rise and fall of his chest. His breathing was slightly labored. She knew she was the cause, and the knowledge excited her. She was succumbing to the intoxication of the moment, she thought dimly. She was falling victim to the physical attraction, and she was undoubtedly making a big mistake. She considered her surroundings and decided the mistake would most likely be little as opposed to big. It would be incredibly uncomfortable and next to impossible to make a big mistake in a Porsche. Actually, his Porsche was sort of an automotive chastity belt, she decided. It was the ideal setting to indulge in an exploratory kiss and not have to worry about losing control of the situation. "Well," she said.

Her voice was husky and slightly breathless, and Pete felt the single word hanging in the air between them, fat and pregnant with erotic potential. "Well," he said back, unsure what to do next, afraid if he moved too fast, his fantasy-come-true would pop like a soap bubble.

Louisa curled her fingers into Pete's jacket and pulled him within inches. He looked like a kid who'd been told he could have ice cream for supper and didn't believe it. "So," she said, "all smoke and no fire, huh?"

"I was under the impression you didn't want fire."

She leaned forward until their noses almost

touched. "I was under the impression you didn't care what I wanted. This is a heck of a time to get sensitive."

He had his seat back, and Louisa on his lap faster than she could formulate a protest. His hand moved under her coat, under her shirt, flesh to heated flesh, and his mouth covered hers in a kiss that made no effort at restraint. There was fire there, all right. More than she'd expected. Much more than she'd actually wanted. Their tongues tangled, his hand moved higher, and in a flash of panic, Louisa realized this wasn't the first time Pete Streeter had made a mistake in his Porsche—and the size of the present mistake was much larger than she'd originally anticipated. It was the last coherent thought she had before passion took over. After that moment there was only heat and need and aching desire. She writhed in his arms as his fingers stroked and inflamed her. She struggled with her clothes and whimpered in despair and delight when his mouth left hers to move lower. But she'd been right. Union was awkward in the cramped quarters.

Five

"Hold it," Louisa said. "I don't think this is gonna work."

Pete had reached the same conclusion, but he wasn't willing to give up so easily. "Let's just roll out into the woods."

"I'm not rolling around in the woods! It's freezing out there." Louisa pushed her tangled hair back from her face and struggled to regain some focus. It had all happened so fast. She was naked, and she was in an obscenely embarrassing position with her foot stuck in the steering wheel. She looked down at herself and groaned. "How did I manage to get my clothes off in this tiny car?"

His grin widened as he snagged her panties from the rearview mirror. "It was nothing short of a miracle. You were a desperate woman."

She snatched her panties from him and tried

to extricate her foot, feeling the humiliation crawling up her spine, burning her earlobes. If she lived through this, she'd be a changed woman, she promised herself. She'd turn celibate for life, and she'd never again ride in a Porsche. Right now, her most pressing need was to get both feet on the floor. "I think I have a problem here," she said, twisting her foot this way and that, having no luck at wriggling it free.

Pete didn't think it was a problem. As far as he was concerned, she could stay in that position for the next sixty years. He'd never seen anything so sexy in his entire life, and he hadn't exactly been a choirboy.

"Well, for crying out loud," Louisa said. "Do something!" Here she was strung up like the Christmas goose, and Pete was just sitting there staring at her.

He smiled silkily and slid his hands up the insides of her thighs.

"That's not going to help." She gasped. "It's my ankle that's stuck!"

"No need to shout. You weren't specific about what I should do. Besides, this is very enticing." He brushed his fingertips over a part of her that was slick and warm and dark in shadow.

Louisa groaned. His touch was lovely, but her foot was falling asleep, and her modesty was asserting itself. She was naked, and Pete Streeter was completely clothed. Five minutes earlier she'd approved of that arrangement; at the present moment she'd be grateful if she could just drop off the face of the earth. She gave a small moan.

"My toes are numb. My foot's going to have to be amputated."

Pete sighed. He didn't want her foot to be amputated, but damned if he didn't like looking at her with her leg hooked up onto the dashboard. "I'll help you get loose, but we'll have to do this again sometime," he said, inching her foot through the opening in the wheel.

"When hell freezes over. This has been the most embarrassing night of my life. Let me get my clothes on, and then push me out the door. When you get home you can send a cab to come get me. I don't ever want to see you again. I'm moving to Montana tomorrow. Maybe I'll be a cowboy. Do they still have cowboys?" She searched under the seat. "I'm missing a sock."

"Moving to Montana isn't a good idea. You'd miss the air pollution, the traffic jams, the lines at the supermarket checkout. I think you should stay here. We could get married."

"I don't want to get married. The only thing I want to get is dressed. And I'm never taking my clothes off again. Not ever. Not even when I take a shower."

He didn't understand her embarrassment. It wasn't as if they were strangers. They'd just almost made love. True, it hadn't been exactly as he'd imagined their first lovemaking would be, but he thought it should count for something. Maybe that was the problem, he decided. They had gone too fast, been too frantic. They should try it again, slowly, with tender words and maddeningly gentle touches. He looked down at his jeans. He could do it. Watching her gather her clothes had reinspired him. Her breasts were still bare, the tips still rosy and swollen. More inspiration.

She worked at untangling her bra from the gearshift, and her breasts jiggled with the effort. That tears it, Pete thought. A man could only take so much. "I don't want you to feel awkward," he said, popping the top snap on his jeans. "The problem here is that I have too many clothes on, so I'll take some off."

"I don't care what you do with *your* clothes," Louisa told him, shoving her arms into her shirt. "I'm keeping mine on for the rest of my life, and I'm going to try very hard to forget this happened."

He shook his head. Women were such a puzzle . . . especially this woman. He debated apologizing, but discarded the idea. He didn't feel apologetic. He felt affectionate and proprietary. He also felt a tad insulted that Louisa wasn't responding in kind and wanted to forget the whole thing. "Participants are supposed to get mellow after almost making love. Where's your afterglow? Where's your sense of humor?"

"That wasn't almost making love. That was . . ." She searched for a word but couldn't come up with anything horrible enough. All the words that came to mind were shamefully exultant. In truth, it had been hands down the most exciting ten minutes of her life. It had been excruciatingly delicious. That didn't alter the fact that she was now mortally embarrassed and disgusted with herself. "That was a conflagration," she finally said.

He smiled in agreement. It had indeed been a conflagration.

She tugged her navy cords over her hips. "It must have been the seltzer. Maybe it was the moon. Is there a full moon out tonight?"

"This is insulting."

Louisa shrugged into her jacket. When she was fully clothed she turned and looked at him. His face was unreadable in the darkness, but she could see enough to know he wasn't smiling. His tone had become serious and chillingly quiet. Now *he* was mad, she realized. She supposed he had reason to be. Blaming her passion on the moon wasn't flattering to him. It also wasn't true, but the truth wasn't something she wanted to face right now. "I suppose physical attraction might have played a part."

"Uh-huh."

He didn't look appeased. She sighed and slouched in her seat. "What do you want from me, Streeter?"

"How about the truth?"

"I wouldn't tell you the truth if you beat me senseless. You could rip off my fingernails, dunk me in boiling oil, carve your initials on my forehead . . ."

He made a disgusted sound. "Stop. You're making me nauseous." He took the keys from the ignition and jerked his thumb at her door. "Out."

"I was only kidding about taking a cab," Louisa said: "You aren't going to make me take a cab, are you?"

"No. I'm going to make you look for a pig. I'd hate for you to have to write this night off as a complete loss."

There was a short patch of grass slanting away from the road. Beyond the grass was a birch stand. Pete set off into the birch stand, and Louisa scrambled to keep up. Beyond the birch stand was a brick-and-aluminum colonial on a quarter of an acre of mostly open lawn. The house seemed austere in the moonlight. Rectangles of light spilled onto the ground from downstairs windows.

Pete didn't care about the colonial. Pete was interested in the weathered rambler next door. Bucky Dunowski lived in the rambler. There was a big Ford pickup in Bucky's gravel drive, a Harley parked on the front porch, and a union jack hung from the sagging porch roof. A dog barked in the vicinity of the rambler.

"That's it," Louisa said. "I'm out of here."

Pete held fast to her. "The dog's chained, Wimpy."

"It isn't that I'm afraid," Louisa insisted. "It's just that I don't see any pigs. We may as well go home."

Someone shouted into the darkness for the dog to shut up, but the dog continued to bark. The back door to the rambler opened, the dog hurried inside, and the door slammed closed.

Pete pulled Louisa forward. "I thought this was important to you."

"That was before I decided to move to Montana."

"Where's your spirit of adventure? And what about outrage. Someone smashed your car windows. You've been fired, and there are clandestine activities afoot in the Senate chambers."

She dug her heels in halfway across the lawn. "My car is insured."

"That doesn't make this pig fiasco any less outrageous."

"*This* is outrageous," she said, flapping her arms. "I feel compelled to point out to you that it is not considered polite behavior to go sneaking around at night, peeking in people's windows."

He motioned for her to be quiet while he crept closer to the house. The muted sound of a television carried out to them. Beer cans and take-out cartons littered the ground around a garbage can on the back stoop. Bars of yellow light bordered either side of a shade drawn on a front window. There were three windows on the driveway side of the house where Pete and Louisa stood. The forward window was shaded and lit. The middle and back windows were dark with shades partially drawn. Pete and Louisa squinted through the grime on the middle window. Enough ambient light spilled from the front room to make out a card table and folding chairs. A door opened to the back room, which Pete assumed was the kitchen. A wide arch connected the middle room with the front room. A man slouched in a worn-out easy chair, his face illuminated by the flickering glow from the television. He was about six feet and stocky, dressed in jeans and a dark T-shirt. The arm facing Louisa and Pete was heavily tatooed. His hair was black, cut short. He had a large Band-Aid taped across the bridge of his nose and a bad bruise running the length of his cheek.

"Bet I know how he got that broken nose," Pete whispered.

"Obviously, you gave better then you got," Louisa said.

Peter grinned at the pride in her voice. There was hope for her. "I don't see any pigs."

"Not the four-legged kind," she said. She stepped back from the window and accidentally kicked a beer can. It skittered over packed dirt onto the gravel drive. Bucky lunged out of the easy chair, and a big black German shepherd materialized from somewhere in the house and flung himself, snarling and snapping, against the dining room window.

Pete grabbed Louisa's hand and took off across the neighboring lawn. They were running flat out when they heard two blasts from a shotgun. Rear lights went on in the colonial. The shepherd was baying behind them, and Pete glanced over his shoulder to see the dog closing in. Two more shotgun blasts peppered the ground to their right. They hit the birch stand just as the back door to the colonial was flung open and a rottweiler bounded out. There was a yelp followed by an awful racket that spun Pete around in his tracks.

Louisa held tight to Pete, gasping for breath. "What *is* it?"

"Looks to me like both houses let their dogs loose at the same time, and they've attacked each other."

Louisa peered out from the patch of trees. Two men had waded, kicking and swearing, into the melee. The dogs were untangled, and swearing gave way to accusations and to hand gestures. Suddenly, the rottweiler's owner stopped arguing and pointed toward the thicket where Pete and Louisa stood obscured in the shadows. Bucky shouldered his shotgun.

"Uh-oh," Pete said. He grabbed Louisa by the wrist and dragged her, full sprint, through the woods to the car. He shoved her inside, scrambled behind the wheel, and took off, spraying gravel behind him and laying a sixteenth of an inch of rubber on the blacktop.

They were past Frederick, Maryland, before Louisa was able to speak. Her heart was still pounding in her chest and perspiration trickled down her breastbone. She lay back in her seat, eyes closed, hand to her forehead. "Holy cow," she said.

Pete's mental exclamation was much stronger. If it hadn't been for the rottweiler, they'd be dog food right now. He was going to have to be more careful. He'd almost gotten Louisa killed. He needed to go home, pour himself a drink, and review the game plan.

Five more minutes of silence passed. They were on Route 280, heading south. Louisa finally opened her eyes. "I'm not cut out for this. I'm a failure as a peeper."

"You just haven't had enough practice. You were doing great until you punted the beer can."

She studied him for a moment and realized he wasn't rattled by the chase. His voice was steady with a hint of humor. His hand was relaxed on the wheel. His cavalier attitude piqued her interest. "How come I'm the only one sweating? Why aren't your hands shaking like mine?"

"I'm big and brave."

"This isn't the first time you've been shot at, is it?"

"Hell no," he said. "I used to drive the freeway to work."

"I'm serious."

He glanced over at her. "I wrote my first screenplay six years ago while I was recovering from a gunshot wound."

"Angry husband?"

"Angry drug runner. I was a Central American correspondent for Reuters, and I was tagging along with some Special Forces guys who were supposed to blow up an airstrip in El Salvador. I caught a bullet in the leg. It shattered the bone and pretty much ended my ability to tramp through the jungle."

Her eyebrows raised a half inch. "How long were you in Central America working for Reuter?"

"Almost four years."

"Covering drug runners, riots, and minor wars?"

He nodded.

"And you were shot at a lot?"

"Not a lot." Looking at it in retrospect, he thought his chances of dying from a firefight back then had been considerably less than his chances of dying from alcohol poisoning. It was hard to believe he'd achieved such success writing screenplays. His personal history wasn't exactly impressive. He'd been a lousy student with a rotten attitude. He'd been caught stealing cars when he was eighteen and joined the army to avoid jail. He'd been the world's worst soldier, getting busted down for everything from insubordination to impersonating an officer. He'd started his newspaper career on the loading dock, sweated his way into the mail room, and farther up. He'd made progress as a correspondent, because he was good, but he never followed the rules and was a thorn in everyone's side. People were willing to give him glowing recommendations with the hope that he'd move on to another job. He suspected his boss at Reuters had sent him to Central America to get him out of the office. Somewhere along the line, looking at life from the bottom of a bottle in Central America, he'd managed to grow up. And he'd discovered a code of ethics and a level of responsibility he could live with.

Louisa considered this latest piece of information. Reuters was a very respectable news service. She hadn't thought much about Pete's background up until now. Certainly, she hadn't envisioned him as a hard-edge journalist tagging after a bunch of mercenaries. Still, it seemed in keeping with his character, and she could easily imagine him with a three-day-old beard and filthy, sweaty clothes, tramping through the jungle, rooting out crime and corruption. She was sure when he was a kid he'd never backed down from a dare, and as a journalist she thought he must have been as single-minded as a mongrel with a soup bone once he'd latched on to a story. That was why he was picking away at this pig thing, she thought. He had the instincts of a journalist. He knew when something was rotten. And he knew when there was a story out there, waiting to be told to the world.

The more she thought about it, the more exotic and heroic it seemed, and her life sounded dull in comparison. She'd lived all her life within the beltway. She'd barely traveled because she'd never had time for a vacation. She'd never seen a jungle or a desert or even the Pacific Ocean. In the past, she'd never much cared about seeing Kuala Lumpur or San Salvador or Shagai Fort, but suddenly she felt rabid with wanderlust. She should broaden her horizons, she thought. She should see more of the world. Maybe she should get a job with the CIA or Cunard or join the Peace Corps.

She was on adrenaline overload, she acknowledged. She was romanticizing Pete Streeter, and she was grossly exaggerating her desire to trade modern plumbing for a glimpse of the Khyber Pass. Still, she felt exhilarated over the idea that, suddenly, there were all sorts of new options and exciting experiences available to her.

Pete went east on the beltway to Connecticut and then cut south. He wasn't sure if it was the best route, but it seemed the most straightforward. Louisa probably knew of a better road, but he didn't want to disturb her. She was lost in thought, chewing his last stick of gum for all she was worth. Her cheeks were flushed, and her hair was wild and tangled. She was steamy from passion and their run through the woods. She smelled like sex and Juicy Fruit, and just sitting next to her made his heart race. She was primordial woman in a Porsche. She was beautiful and erotic and naively blind to the power she held over him. He couldn't imagine what she was thinking, but the next morning she was going to wake up with her blood pressure back to normal and the passion of the night hours behind her. She was going to be furious that she'd almost made it in a car, on the side of a road, with a man she'd only known for three days and thought was a notch below slug spit. He was going to keep his door locked and his sound system cranked up until she was done breaking things.

He left Connecticut with its neon-lit restaurants and twenty-four-hour traffic. A block off Connecticut on 27th Street, urban Washington was dark and quiet, settled in for the night behind locked doors. Globed streetlights dropped dim light over gray sidewalk and made the porch and shrub shadows seem black and deep.

Pete always felt comfortable here. There was a softness to 27th Street. It was unpretentious with its old-fashioned above-ground wires, rickety garages, and messy lawns. The residents were busy but not unfriendly. His house in Santa Barbara had privacy because of the exclusivity of the neighborhood. His Manhattan condo had privacy because the doorman strictly enforced it. 27th Street was a place where privacy needn't be guarded. Privacy occurred naturally on 27th Street through a lack of interest and a shortage of idle hours. There was normalcy here, Pete thought. It was a place to raise children and grow old with grace. At least, it had been prior to the pig business.

Pete parked the car and followed Louisa to her door and into her apartment. He checked out each room, including the closets. He made sure the windows were locked and the back door secure. The following day the alarm system would be in place. For the night he'd have to hope for the best. "It would be safer if we stayed together tonight," he said.

Louisa weighed the risk of being attacked in her sleep and decided she was safer taking her chances with the pig people. "I don't think that's a good idea."

"I'd sleep on the couch."

Louisa rolled her eyes.

"Unless you'd rather I slept in your bed . . ."

She felt the flush creeping up from her shirt collar. "I don't want to talk about it."

Pete grinned. He pulled her to him and kissed

her long and hard. When he was done, he sighed in satisfaction. "Still hot for me, huh?"

He was right, of course, and that made it all the worse. "Out," Louisa said. "Out, out, out, out, out!"

He gave another sigh. This time it was clearly regret. He let himself out the front door and stood on the porch until he heard the lock click.

Louisa wasn't sure she wanted to get out of bed. It was morning, and the sun was shining, and Washington was on the move without her. She had no place to go—no job, no future. Even if she had a place to go, she couldn't go there because she still hadn't gotten her car repaired.

The beaches of Belize no longer beckoned. Only one memory held vibrant in her mind. She'd almost done *it* with Pete Streeter in his Porsche. She buried her face in her pillow and screamed. She was a slut, no doubt about it. Even worse, she was a *dumb* slut. Getting involved with Pete Streeter was dumb and would bring her nothing but grief. She groaned. Who was she kidding. She already was involved.

Okay, what could she do about it? The only thing that came to mind was suicide. The more she thought about it, the more appealing it became. The method of death would have to be lingering and pathetic, she decided. She wanted to suffer. She wanted to be an object of pity. Guns were too gory. A knife would be too painful. Pills might make her throw up. She could drive off the Woodrow Wilson Bridge, but first she'd have to rent a car. Hanging didn't sound like fun. She didn't want her eyes to bulge out of her head. Starvation was the way to go, she finally concluded. She would simply lay in bed and waste away.

She went back to sleep and awoke again at nine-thirty. She was hungry, but she supposed she had to get used to it if she was going to starve to death. She was examining a crack in her ceiling when she heard someone pounding on her front door. Ignore it, she told herself, but the knocking was relentless. It intruded on her self-indulgent depression. She lurched out of bed and shoved her arms into her robe. She went to the front door and threw it open. It was Pete Streeter. "Yes?"

He handed her the morning paper and a big white bakery bag and eased past her into her apartment. "I figured you'd be bummed out this morning, so I brought you some doughnuts."

She stared nonplussed at the bag. Here she was trying to kill herself, and Streeter had brought her doughnuts. Damn. "So," she said, "what kind of doughnuts?"

"All kinds. I didn't know what you liked so I got four of everything."

"Boston creams?"

"Fresh made this morning. They're right on top so the icing doesn't get smeared."

Okay, she thought, she'd starve to death tomorrow. She had lots of time. There was no rush. She took a Boston cream and chomped off a big bite. Might as well make coffee since she wasn't going to do the suicide thing, she told herself. She padded into the kitchen and put a pot of water on to boil.

Pete tagged along and slouched in a kitchen chair. Her hair was a mess and her robe was unbelted, revealing a flannel nightgown that would have discouraged a lesser man. He thought she looked great. "You sleep okay?" he asked.

"Yep."

"I expected you'd be up and dressed by now."

"I was in the early stages of death by somnolence, but you disturbed me."

"There's always tomorrow."

"Exactly," she said, finishing off her first doughnut, selecting a second. Maybe she wouldn't starve to death, she decided. Maybe she'd eat herself into obesity and explode. Death by doughnut.

"Have plans for the day?"

"Nothing past these doughnuts." She made the coffee, poured two cups, and gave one to Pete.

He took a piece of lined paper from his shirt pocket. "I made a list of things we should do."

"If any of this involves taking my clothes off, you can forget it."

"Undressing is optional."

She looked at the list. "You want me to proofread your rewrites?"

"I can't spell, and I don't have time to use the spell check on the computer. Then I want you to systematically call all your Capitol Hill friends and catch up on gossip. Try to steer the conversation around to pigs and Stu Maislin."

"What are you going to do while I'm gossiping?"

"I'm going back to Pennsylvania. I want to take a look at the pig farm. Then I'm meeting a friend for lunch." He downed his coffee and stood. "Horowitz Security is supposed to show up sometime this morning. They'll be working on both apartments." He tossed a key onto the table. "This is for my front door." He thought about kissing her but decided against it. She didn't look as if she wanted to be kissed, and she had her mouth full of jelly doughnut. "See you later."

She had a third doughnut in her hand. "Mmmphf."

Six

It was twelve-thirty when Pete pushed his way into the McDonald's on K Street. Kurt New-farmer was already there. He was sitting in a front booth with what looked to be a firebreak around him. He wasn't the sort of man people naturally gravitated toward.

Pete got a coffee and joined him, counting up the cartons and crumpled wrappers on the table. "Two Big Macs, one fish filet, three large fries, McNuggets, and a chocolate shake. Not hungry?"

"Watching my waistline."

They were the same age, late thirties, but Kurt's brown hair had already started to recede, and what was left had been cut in a Marine Corps buzz. Kurt Newfarmer was six feet with a corded neck and tightly muscled body that looked deceptively lean and loose. He was wearing a grimy ball cap, grimy jeans, running shoes, and a hooded sweatshirt of indeterminate color. Stained thermal underwear showed at the neck of the sweatshirt. He had a three-day-old beard, his eyes were lined and narrow, and years ago his nose had been reshaped by a gun butt. He reminded Pete of a down-and-out homeless hundred-and-eighty-pound ferret.

Pete had first met Kurt when he was in El Salvador, and Kurt had been the signal man for a ranger unit. Kurt was a communications genius. Two years ago he'd quit the army and started doing free-lance wiretap. It was rumored he was also semi-officially on the payroll for one of the three-word agencies. "I've got a problem," Pete said.

"Don't we all."

Pete pointed to his eye. The swelling had gone down, but he had a classic shiner. "Three days ago this problem broke into my house."

"I like the part along the bridge of your nose that's turning green," Kurt said.

Pete knew Kurt had him pegged as a bad apple. Pete figured that was pretty funny since next to Kurt he thought he looked like Mr. Rogers. "I might need some help."

Kurt gave the bulge under his left armpit a pat. "Just tell Uncle Kurt, and he'll take care of it."

"Must be awkward to get at your gun with that sweatshirt on."

"Hell, I hardly ever use it. It's been days since I've shot at anyone." Kurt took a cigarette from the pack on the table and lit up. He dragged smoke into his lungs until there was a half inch of glowing ash at the end of his Camel. Smoke curled from his nose and rolled out the side of his mouth. He squinted at Pete through the haze. "So what's going on? Bummed out husband?"

Pete felt dizzy with nicotine deprivation. He automatically leaned forward to catch the secondary smoke, caught himself in midlean, and reluctantly shoved himself away.

Kurt caught the movement. "Trying to stop smoking again?"

"Could you look like you're enjoying it a little less."

The grin broadened. "It's great, man."

"You available for hire?"

"What do you want done?"

"For starters, I want to listen to a couple of people."

"You've come to the right place."

Louisa sat at her kitchen table and stared out her back window. There was a small gray bird sitting on her bird feeder. It wasn't eating, it wasn't preening, it wasn't chirping. It was just hunkered down, its feet automatically clamped onto the wood dowel. Louisa supposed it was wondering what to do next. She was in a similar state. She was the firstborn in her family and like most first children, she'd been the achiever. She'd been the honor roll student, the responsible daughter, the first to graduate college. Despite all this, her sense of purpose had never been well defined. For all her intelligence and discipline, she'd been a drifter. She'd made the major decisions of her life by default. She'd worked hard to excel at whatever task was before her, but she'd never charted a course for herself. She'd never felt impassioned about a career choice, so she'd simply traveled the path of least resistance. It hadn't been so bad, she thought. But it hadn't been great, either. At best, it had paid the rent and kept her too busy to dwell on the fact that her life lacked zest. Looking at it in retrospect, she decided her life had been . . . adequate.

All that had changed since she'd met Peter Streeter. Peter Streeter was to her life what the big bang had been to the creation of the universe. She imagined herself as traveling in a new orbit, amid cataclysmic forces. Plague, pestilence, volcanic destruction were now hers for the asking.

She continued to watch the bird, feeling a special kinship, wondering at his next move. He could be contemplating a flight to Florida, or debating a love affair. He could be wrestling with a dinner choice, reviewing bird feeders of the past, recalling gourmet sunflower seeds and suet balls. Maybe his head was filled with dreams of foreign lands, just as hers had been the night before. "Go for it," she said to the bird. "Take a chance! What have you got to lose?"

The bird cocked his head and smoothed

fluffed feathers. Then he took off from the porch and smacked into the kitchen window.

Louisa jumped out of her chair and ran out the back door. The bird was laying on the frozen ground with his head at an odd angle and his bird feet uncommonly limp. Louisa felt time stand still for several seconds while she stared at the bird. She could see his heart beating under his breastbone. His eyes were open but unfocused. Several more seconds passed and the bird started flopping around, staggering a few steps and falling over. He stopped staggering, sat very still, and rested a bit. Finally he flew away.

"Damn stupid bird," Louisa said.

She turned and found she was locked out of her house. Ordinarily she'd have jimmied the kitchen window, but the new alarm system was on, and her apartment was as secure as the Louvre.

Each of the row houses had a small backyard, enclosed with a privacy fence, which sloped up to a narrow, pockmarked macadam alleyway. Houses on the other side of the alley had ramshackled wood, single-car garages. Louisa's side wasn't so affluent. Louisa's side only had room for garbage cans. To get to the front of her house she had to let herself out the back gate, walk down the macadam lane for four-house lengths to a driveway connecting the lane to 27th Street and 28th Street. She gave her doorknob one more try, but it was useless. It was definitely locked. She kicked the door and swore. Then she looked around to see if anyone was watching. No. No one was home on either side of her. Everyone worked. Everyone but her. She didn't think Pete Streeter counted as legitimate employment. She swore again and hustled up to the alley, saying a fervent prayer that by some act of God her front door wouldn't be locked.

Pete pulled up to the curb just as she was approaching their house. She had her mouth set into a grim line, her nose was red from the cold, and she had her shoulders hunched and her arms wrapped across her chest. No coat. No hat. No gloves. It wasn't hard to figure out. "How'd it happen?" he asked.

"Some idiot bird crashed into my kitchen window, and I went out to see if he was okay."

"Ahh."

She stood her ground in silent obstinacy, mentally daring him to make a wisecrack.

"So, did kamikaze bird go to the big bird farm in the sky?"

"Flew off without so much as a chirp."

"The front door locked too?"

"Probably."

He took his jacket off and stuffed her into it. "Wait in the Porsche where it's warm. I'll see if I can get in." A few moments later he returned and slid behind the wheel. He tapped a number into the car phone and explained to Horowitz that he was locked out. "They're on their way," he told Louisa.

"You don't suppose the bird was prophetic, do you?" she asked Streeter. "I mean, it couldn't

possibly be the word of God, making a statement to the effect of bashing one's head against
a brick wall, or trying to fly to unrealistic heights,
could it?"

"What kind of bird was it?"

"A little gray bird."

"Definitely not the word of God. God uses big
birds to send messages. Condors and eagles.
Maybe an occasional albatross. Your little gray
bird probably forgot to put his contacts in when
he got up this morning."

Louisa wasn't so sure. "I don't know," she
said. "It has to make you think."

Pete looked at her and decided she was a
woman at a crossroads. "He didn't actually hurt
himself," Pete said.

"But he could have."

"But he *didn't*."

They stared at each other, and they knew they
weren't talking about birds. Pete was a risk
taker, and all her life she'd been risk adverse.
The previous night change had sounded exciting. Now it was intimidating. What was right for
Pete Streeter wasn't necessarily right for her. He
was his own person. She'd spent a few hours
that morning at the library, reading back issues
of the trades. She'd discovered there was very
little written about Pete's personal life and early
childhood. He was obviously a much more private person than she'd originally thought. He
was also much more wealthy. Good screenplay
writers were well rewarded, and Pete Streeter
seemed to be one of the best. Screenplay writers

also enjoyed less recognition by the public than other members of the movie community. She'd seen all his movies, yet she hadn't recognized his name when he'd introduced himself four days before. When she'd done a mental review of his movies, she'd been able to reach a few perfunctory observations on style. All movies had content. All movies were fast paced, filled with action, laced with humor. He had a decided preference for political thrillers. He'd been nominated for an Academy Award three times. One nomination had resulted in an Oscar. And as they were known to say in Hollywood, Streeter was big box office. His movies had all been financially successful.

He'd put a lot of himself into his screenplays, she'd decided. Under all that incredible hair was intelligence and sensitivity and an understanding of human nature. She also recognized that her judgment of him might be colored by his ability to inspire passion, the likes of which she'd never before experienced. It wasn't enough to make her want to spend the rest of her life with him, but she didn't want to minimize the accomplishment, either.

She wasn't ready to deal with her conflicting, rapidly changing feelings for Streeter, so she turned the conversation back to business. "Did you find anything interesting in Pennsylvania?"

"It'd be easier to get into CIA headquarters in Langley than to break into that pig farm. The place is surrounded by an electrified fence and razor wire. I only got as far as the front gate.

They don't give guided tours, and the guard wasn't impressed with my Mr. Charm routine."

"Low cholesterol bacon is very high tech."

"How about you? You have any luck?"

"I got three invitations to lunch and found out Beverly Kootz is having an affair with her hairdresser."

"Anything else?"

"Nolan hired a new press secretary. Some bimbo from New York. Worked in broadcasting. Supposedly has a lot of contacts. Rumor has it, she's been seen going in and out of motel rooms with Stu Maislin."

Pete leaned closer so he could smell her hair. "The plot thickens."

"Mmmm. I think Nolan probably owed Maislin a favor, and they used my association with you as an excuse to give the slut a job."

"Nasty."

"Hey, that's life."

"You're being very philosophical about this," Pete said.

"Getting fired has forced me to reexamine my life."

"Did it come up short?"

She thought about it a moment. "Not exactly short. Maybe a little undernourished."

"Needed a kick in the pants?"

Louisa laughed. "Yeah. Something like that."

He'd promised himself there'd be no more groping in a car, and he decided it was going to be a damn hard promise to keep. They'd only been sitting together for a short time, but already he could feel the pressure growing behind the zipper of his jeans. It was nothing compared to the ache in his heart, he ruefully admitted. He was besotted. He wasn't sure how it had happened, only that he'd been hit fast and hard. It had started out as an innocent physical attraction, had quickly grown into an amusing infatuation, and then the virus had skyrocketed out of control. He could feel affection and desire multiplying exponentially inside him. Two hours earlier he'd been able to joke about being in love. Now it had him by the short hairs.

He should be watching for Horowitz, he thought, but Louisa was silky and warm beside him. He ran his thumb along the line of her jaw and watched her lips part in expectation of a kiss. He suspected she wasn't going to be much help with the groping problem. He wasn't completely unhappy about that, he admitted. He twirled a curl around his finger while he debated if he should tell her his feelings. "Listen, Lou, there's something I need to tell you. It's about last night . . ."

"Last night was possibly the most embarrassing night of my life. I don't know what came over me! I attacked you, for crying out loud!"

"Yeah. You were great."

"I don't want to talk about it."

"You don't want to talk about the way you tore at your clothes until you were sprawled across my lap completely naked?"

"Exactly. That's exactly what I don't want to talk about."

He nuzzled her neck. "Or the way you offered your breasts to me and moaned when I teased the nipples until they were hard and aching?"

Louisa bit down on her lower lip.

He pinned her to the seat and slid his hands under her shirt. "Lord, Lou, you're so hot."

"How do you know?"

He smiled like the cat that just swallowed the canary, and passed his thumb over the already aroused tip of her breast. "Men know these things."

A thrill ripped through her at his touch, and with it came panic. "Just what do you think you're doing?"

"Demonstrating. I have a visual aid, too, if you're interested."

"No!" She knew exactly what visual aid the man was talking about. It was straining the seam of his jeans. Thank goodness they made jeans like iron these days, she thought. If it had been an inferior pair, his visual aid looked like it might burst right through. "This is a respectable neighborhood," she told him. "People don't go around using visual aids in broad daylight here. It's illegal, I think." He was still manipulating the tight little nub at the end of her breast, and she was finding it difficult to breath, difficult to remember why she didn't want to see his visual aid. He kissed her deeply, using his tongue and his teeth, not bothering to hide the extent of his need, and reality whirled away from her. There was only Pete and the enslaving sensations he produced in her body. There was lust, red-hot and bawdy, and there was a sweet excitement, a premonition that she was about to fly off in a million new directions through uncharted space.

A sharp rap on the driver's side window broke into the kiss, and Louisa was dimly aware of Pete pulling away and swearing softly. It took a moment for her to realize Horowitz had arrived.

"I'm from Horowitz Security," the man said when Pete rolled down the window. "You the people that's locked outta the house? Nice to see you're putting your time to good use."

"Trying to keep warm," Pete said.

"Looks like it's working."

Five minutes later Pete and Louisa were alone in Louisa's apartment. Pete closed the front door and reactivated the system. "Now, where were we before Horowitz . . ."

Louisa narrowed her eyes and tapped her foot. "Where is it?"

"Where's what?"

"Don't play dumb with me." She looked down the front of her shirt. "My bra is missing. Where is it?"

He pulled it out of his pocket.

"How did you do that? I have all the rest of my clothes on! How did it get into your pocket without my suspecting?"

"It's an innate talent."

"You're a despicable person," she said. "You're a real scuzzball."

His hands were tangled in her hair, and his lips were very close to hers. "You don't mean that." His lips brushed over her mouth; his voice hummed, softly resonant, against her ear. "I think you're beginning to like me."

"Maybe a little."

He kissed her lightly. Then he kissed her again with much more feeling. He'd do it right this time, he thought. He swept her into his arms and carried her into the bedroom. His hands inflamed as they undressed. When she was naked, he took his mouth to her, covering her with kisses that were achingly gentle and supremely intimate. She moaned low in her throat and writhed against the rising tide of desire.

He was still fully clothed. He was afraid to love her any other way. Even if she begged, and he could see she was close, he was determined not to rush, not to let his own passion set the pace. Her skin was flushed, her breasts and lips swollen from his kisses. His hand pressed into the moist heat between her legs, his thumb rubbed over her pubic bone. He felt her shudder, and his fingers found the slick, tumescent core of her womanhood.

Never had she wanted a man like this. She was burning with a hunger she'd never even suspected existed. The previous night she'd felt all explosive energy and a need that was frantic and furious and frighteningly powerful. This was slow, relentless heat, inexorable, unescapable. Every inch of her skin was aroused, her blood felt hot and thick in her veins, her pulse beat to the rhythm set by her lover's touch. She itched for release and was sure she could no longer bear the exquisite torture. But it continued, and, impossible as it seemed, the intensity increased. She heard herself panting, begging, crying out at each new stab of pleasure. She lifted up to him, greedy for more, all modesty discarded. She was stripped bare, her basest needs exposed, and she reveled in the freedom such exposure brought.

He stood, peeled off his clothes, pinned her hands to the bed, and mounted her, pressing deep inside with painstaking care. The sense of union was overwhelming, taking his breath away, causing him to pause for a moment.

She dragged her eyes open. He was beautiful. His expression was one of rapt attention and tender affection. She could spend a lifetime looking at his face, she thought. A lifetime of loving him and being loved. She would never tire of him, never grow bored, never stop wanting him. She watched the control slip from him, saw his eyes darken as passion gained the upper hand. He bore down on her, and she felt the bite of fire, felt the pressure instantly push her to the edge. And then she was gone, taking him with her, hurtling through time and space, lost in that all-encompassing velvet blackness only perfectly matched lovers know.

They lay together for a long time afterward in companionable silence. It had been better than death by doughnut, she thought. And she was definitely happy she hadn't died of starvation. She suspected this was one of those moments in time, like daybreak, when the world held its breath, crossed its fingers, and made promises. She didn't care. It was lovely, all the same, and she allowed herself the luxury of feeling in love.

They crawled under the quilt and snuggled into each other, finding they were newly aroused. This time the loving was relaxed. This time they loved with smiles and whispered words, secure in their ability to please. Their climax was a celebration of their new alliance. It was an affirmation of a loving friendship, filled with the joy of shared intimacies.

Overhead, the phone rang once. Louisa forced her eyes open. "Your phone rang."

"The recorder will take it."

"You still getting threatening phone calls?"

"The recorded messages stopped two days ago, but this morning I got an interesting call on my car phone. Stu Maislin told me in no uncertain terms that he wasn't pleased to have me snooping around in his house. He indicated I might lose a part of my anatomy if I continued to harass him."

Louisa propped herself up on one elbow and looked at him. "I'm afraid to ask which part."

"Your favorite."

"Bummer."

Louisa's phone rang in the kitchen.

"Probably your mother," Pete said.

Louisa rolled out of bed. "I'm going to tell her everything."

Pete grabbed for her ankle, but she was too fast.

A moment later she yelled out to him. "It's for you. It's some guy named Kurt. Says you gave him my number." She covered the mouthpiece and lowered her voice. "Who *is* this guy? He sounds like Arnold Schwarzenegger's cousin from New Jersey."

Seven

Louisa pushed her tangled hair back from her face and wished she'd been more insistent about taking a shower after all their lovemaking. It was close to eight. The lights on the Duke Ellington Bridge lobbed by as the Porsche rolled over Rock Creek into Adams-Morgan. "Okay, tell me one more time about this Kurt person."

"I met him when I was working in Central America, and we've stayed in touch."

"He's a friend?"

"Yeah. He's a friend," he said, "sort of."

"And you've hired him to tap Maislin's phone."

Pete slid a glance in her direction, waiting for the inevitable follow-up.

Louisa didn't disappoint him. "Isn't that illegal?"

"Pretty much."

"Just exactly what does 'pretty much' mean?"

He turned onto Columbia Road and the heart of the Hispanic community. "I think Kurt sort of operates on the fringe."

"Uh-huh."

He didn't know how to explain it to her . . . the way you just *knew* about someone. The way he knew about her. It had to do with trust and gut-level feeling. "Kurt's too much of a patriot to be entirely outside of the law. Most likely, he's one of those maverick CIA types." He gave her a reassuring smile. "Technically, Kurt might be considered to be police."

"We're gonna rot in jail."

Pete parked the Porsche in front of an Ethiopian restaurant. "We're not going to rot in jail. Kurt's the only one taking a risk, and believe me, this doesn't rate high on the risk scale for Kurt." He put a proprietary arm around her shoulders. It was cold and most of the restaurant crowd had dispersed. The streets were eerie with artificial light and the kind of late-evening desertion you found in a commuter city. "Here," he said, maneuvering her through the double glass doors of a yellow brick apartment building. There was a small vestibule with a second security door. Mailboxes and intercoms were built into one wall. Pete pressed the button for number 315, no name.

The voice on the intercom was flat and unwelcoming. "Yeah?"

"It's Pete."

Nothing else was said. The security door buzzed open. It was a five-story building with one elevator at the far side of a small lobby. The lobby carpet needed more than cleaning. The walls were painted rent-control-green. Pete shouldered Louisa into the elevator, punched the button to the third floor, and the elevator doors slid closed. The elevator smelled faintly of urine and a burrito.

Louisa imagined this as being the odor of poverty. She imagined substandard apartments with broken plumbing and roach-infested kitchens where immigrant families crowded chockablock, struggling to hold their lives together. They worked as dishwashers and cabdrivers, and many didn't work at all. Some used drugs, some spent their welfare checks on alcohol, some sent their money home to relatives even more impoverished. They were individuals, she thought, each with their own set of dreams, their own set of skills, their own moments of despair. And they were united by a common odor that hung in the stairwells and corridors of government-controlled housing.

Pete also sniffed the air, but his observations didn't wax nearly so profound. Pete decided Kurt had recently used the elevator.

"Why does Kurt live in this apartment building?" Louisa asked. "Doesn't he have any money?"

Pete shrugged. "Guess he likes it here." And it was a place Kurt could become invisible. Not many questions were asked in a building like this. The doors opened to an institutional corridor. Apartment number 315 was to the right, halfway down. Pete knocked and waited patiently while dead bolts were slid free and locks were clicked open. "About Kurt," he said to Louisa, ". . . be careful."

Louisa thought that was an odd thing to say about a friend. "Careful of what?"

"For starters, don't eat anything that isn't cooked to a crisp."

The door swung wide, and Louisa found herself staring down the barrel of a Smith & Wesson forty-five.

Kurt immediately lowered the gun and let it negligently hang at his side. "Sorry," he said at the expression on Louisa's face. "No sense taking chances."

Pete closed the door behind him and relocked it. "This is Louisa."

"I figured," Kurt said.

Louisa swallowed hard. The apartment consisted of living room, galley kitchen, bedroom, and bath. The furniture was utilitarian and clearly wasn't the main focus of Kurt's life. Newspapers littered the floor, clothing was strewn over chairs, crushed beer cans adorned every available surface, and fast-food wrappers gathered in corners like wax paper dust bunnies. Crates of electronic equipment were stacked against walls, an elaborate computer setup hummed in harmony with the refrigerator, and mysterious black boxes were wired to the computer. Switches clicked on, recorders whirred, digital messages flashed on a control console. A red light blinked, indicating a connection had been made, and a woman's voice carried across the room, murmuring softly in Spanish.

"An embassy?" Pete asked.

Kurt clamped a hand to his crotch and yanked his privates up half an inch. "Phone sex. It goes with my cable hookup."

Louisa sunk her teeth into her lip to keep from whimpering. The air was permeated with the aroma of stale cigarette smoke and gun oil. A heavy-duty cardboard carton caught Louisa's eye. It was half in and half out the open bedroom door. Its top had been ripped off. Even from this distance Louisa could see the carton was three-quarters filled with smaller boxes. The lettering on the side of the carton told her it had been packed for shipping with twenty-four boxes of twelve each, ribbed, tipped condoms. Kurt bought bulk. Very thrifty, she told herself. No reason to panic. He was probably a very nice person. It was true, he looked like a serial killer and acted like a flaming pervert, but looks could be deceiving. And after all, he *did* practice safe sex—lots of it.

Kurt ambled to the kitchen and came back with three beers and a large bag of pork rinds. He gave Louisa a beer and the bag and turned his attention to Pete. "I picked up something you might find interesting." He took a tape from the top of his desk, slid it into a recorder, punched rewind and then play. "Maislin made this call at five twenty-seven from his office, private number. It went out to a number in

Kenton, Pennsylvania. The number is listed to a B. Dunowski."

Pete popped the top to his beer and chugged half a can while he listened to Maislin dial. The connection was made, the phone rang three times, and a man answered.

"Hello." The voice was nasal—the sort of voice you'd expect from a man with a broken nose.

"You still have the stuff." It was more a statement than a question.

"Of course I've got the stuff."

"I've made arrangements," Maislin said. "We'll try it again, and this time pick out a healthy pig."

Pete looked at Louisa. "What are they talking about?"

She shrugged. "They're going to try it again."

Kurt rewound the tape. "Seems to me all you dudes gotta do is be there when they do whatever it is they're gonna do for the second time, and you'll know what it was they were trying to do the first time."

Louisa looked at Kurt. He made sense, but she didn't know how they'd accomplish his suggestion. "Easier said than done."

"Shouldn't be too hard," Kurt said. "You have friends in the building. All you have to do is go into Maislin's office, nose around a little, plant a few bugs."

"Bugs? As in clandestine listening devices? Illegal clandestine listening devices?"

"Yeah. Or even better, you could blackmail

Maislin into giving you a job. Then you could really snoop around."

"No way," Pete said. "Forget it."

Louisa glanced over at him. "Why not?"

"Because it would be dangerous, and I don't want you involved."

"Suppose I *want* to be involved?"

Pete slid his empty beer can onto the counter. "In this particular instance, it wouldn't matter what you wanted."

Louisa narrowed her eyes. "You want to explain that to me?"

"Intimacy brings certain privileges and responsibilities."

"Such as?"

"Such as, I know more about this cloak-and-dagger stuff than you do, and you're going to have to defer to my judgment."

This is it, she thought. This is where you make a stand or forever hate yourself for being a wimp. "No."

Now Pete's eyes were narrowed. "What do you mean no?"

"You're not going to tell me what to think, or what to do, or what's too dangerous for me. I have the right to make my own mistakes and screw up my own life. And that's exactly what I intend to do."

Pete looked over at Kurt. "This make any sense to you?"

Kurt opened the bag of pork rinds. "Women."

"Sent by the devil," Pete said.

"Suppose I wanted to blackmail Maislin," Louisa said. "How would I go about it?"

Kurt slouched bonelessly against the counter. "You'd tell him you knew things he might not want spread around. Then you'd tell him how you need a job, and how you're this great 'team' player."

Pete dipped into the bag of pork rinds. "I'm holding you responsible," he said to Kurt. "This was your dumb idea, and you're encouraging her. Anything happens to her, and I'm coming after you."

"Nothing's gonna happen to her. If you're that nervous, we'll let her wear a wire." He pulled a cardboard box out from under his desk and set it on the table. He found a pair of scissors and a roll of surgical tape. He searched through the box and came up with a small piece of plastic with three wires attached. "This is a flat-pack transmitter," he told Louisa. "It's two inches by one inch, weighs less than an ounce, and has an internal microphone." He touched the slim two-inch wire protruding from the top end. "This is the antenna." He attached a six-volt, flat-pack battery to the two wires at the bottom of the transmitter. The battery was about an eighth of an inch thick and three inches square. "The battery gets taped to your stomach, and the transmitter gets wedged into your cleavage. It'll be invisible under your blouse." He flipped a portable receiver to Pete. "You've worked with this stuff before?"

"Yeah," Pete said. "I know how it goes."

They didn't say a word for the entire ride home, but Louisa thought she could hear Pete grinding his teeth in the dark. "It's not good to hold in all that anger," she finally said. "You'll get a hernia."

He parallel parked in front of the house. "I'm not sure it's anger. I don't know what it is. Frustration, maybe. Confusion." He wrenched the car door open. "Okay, so maybe some of it's anger." And a lot of it was wounded pride, but he didn't want to admit to it out loud.

Louisa followed him up the cement stairs. "It isn't going to work, you know."

"The wire?"

"The relationship."

"It was working fine until you got it into your head to play Junior G-man."

It wasn't working fine, she wanted to scream. They might as well be at opposite ends of the earth. The only things they really agreed on were sex positions. And to top it all off, there was Kurt. Kurt was a strange person, living in a disgusting apartment. If that wasn't bad enough, he was doing illegal things. He answered his door with a gun in his hand. And he was Pete's friend! How could she reconcile this? Kurt was a slimeball. She tapped in her security code and inserted her door key. Maybe Pete was a slimeball, too, she thought. Maybe he just hid it better because he had more money.

The following morning Louisa swung through the doors of the Hart Building, wondering what had gone wrong. She'd intended to be firm about not making love. She'd slept in her own bed, alone. She'd gone through all her familiar rituals alone . . . making her coffee, reading the paper. Then when it had come time for Pete to wire her for sound, she'd lost all resolve. He'd popped the top button on her blouse, and she'd gone into sexual hyperdrive. She made a small disgusted sound and slid a glance in his direction. She suspected he'd seduced her as much out of sport as need. He was half a step behind her, with the receiver in his hand and his headset slung around his neck. He winked and smiled, and she felt like strangling him. He stopped to read a plaque on the wall when she turned into Maislin's office.

She'd called ahead to make an appointment, and Stu Maislin was waiting for her. He was a large man with a face like a bulldog and a personality to match. He wore a nine-hundred-dollar suit and a seventy-dollar silk tie with a gravy stain two inches below the knot. He didn't look friendly. He motioned her into his inner office and closed the door behind them.

"So," Maislin said. "Let's talk business."

Louisa unbuttoned her coat and resisted the urge to feel for the transmitter. "I need a job."

"Maybe I don't have any job openings right now."

"Maybe I should look for a job in the Attorney General's office."

"You trying to blackmail me?"

"I'm trying to persuade you that I can be a team player."

He considered her answer and nodded. "You might fit into my office with an attitude like that. I could put you on as an aide."

"An aide would be fine. I can start tomorrow morning."

He gave her a long look. "Real go-getter, aren't you?"

"My rent is due."

"Just don't get too ambitious, you know what I mean?"

The threat inspired a rush of anger. She took a beat to calm herself and gave him a cool smile as silent acknowledgment that she understood his message.

Pete was waiting for her in the hall. He caught the murderous look in her eyes and gave her wide berth. He didn't attempt conversation until they were in the car. "That seemed to go well," he said.

"He's an arrogant bully. He abuses his staff, throws his weight around in Congress like a Mafia don, and has no scruples."

"Anything else?"

"He had a gravy stain on his tie."

"That clinches it," Pete said. "I'm not voting for him."

"You can't vote for him, anyway. You don't live in his state anymore."

"I could move back."

It was a flip answer, but it stirred questions in

Louisa's mind. "Would you ever do that? Go back?"

He didn't need time to think about it. He shook his head. "No. Not to live. I can barely survive a four-hour visit." Nothing had changed, he thought. There was the same feeling of fatalistic impotency, and he hated it with a passion. His father and brothers were old beyond their years. They complained, but saw no reason for change, no opportunity for improvement. His successes were suspect. What had been good enough for his father and grandfather, brothers, cousins, classmates, hadn't been good enough for him. It generated confusion among his friends and relatives. Pete would have preferred resentment. At least resentment was an aggressive emotion.

"Four hours isn't very long."

"Ahhh," he sighed, "it's a lifetime."

Louisa thought the statement held finality and enormous sadness. "Is it that bad?"

"I used to be afraid to take a vacation. I was afraid that if I stopped writing, even for a few days, I'd never get started again. It was much easier to believe in the power of inertia than in my own talent, my own ambition. For a long time, I was afraid to go home, because I was afraid I might stay. Now I simply find going home to be . . . tedious. No one is comfortable with me."

Louisa winced. "I'm sorry."

"I didn't mean to inspire pity. A lot of the

discomfort is my own doing. I could refrain from trying to ram my ideas down the throats of others. It'd go a long way to make me more popular."

"Not your style," Louisa said. "You're a crusader."

He'd never thought about it exactly in those terms, but he supposed she was right. He wasn't sure it was flattering. "Are crusaders annoying?"

"Yes. That's part of their charm."

He parked the car and they got out.

"Do you think I'm different today?" Louisa asked him.

He trailed after her, assessing the hint of her backside under the black wool coat. He looked at her hair, her shoes, her purse. She seemed the same. "Is this a trick question?"

"I *feel* different," she said.

He curled his fingers into her lapels and pulled her very close. "I wouldn't know about that. I haven't felt you yet."

Her jaw went slack. The man had a one-track mind. She gave him a look normally reserved for the perverts who hung out on Fourteenth Street. "Not *that* kind of feel."

He unlocked his door and ushered her into his lobby. "I know what you mean. You're referring to the fact that you're taking charge of your life. You're being a little rebellious and very brave."

"Yes!"

"It isn't so much that you're different. You're still the same person. It's just that you're more of some things and less of others. You're making choices about your personality." He turned her in the direction of his stairs and gave her a little push. "When I was a kid I let my emotions rule me. Whatever I felt was out there for all to see—anger, frustration, childish exuberance. I was self-indulgent, did everything to excess, and was intolerant of anyone who did less. I stole more cars, went out with more girls, drank myself into oblivion at every opportunity, and was the worst student, worst soldier, worst reporter ever. I was also the best student, best soldier, and best damn reporter ever. I was fearless from bloated ego and lack of caring. It took a bullet in the leg and the death of a good friend to slow me down. I made some decisions while I was lying in the hospital. I decided there was some value to restraint, self-discipline, moral responsibility. It seems to me you're coming at it from the other end. Basically we're people with passionate personalities, but you were taught control as a child. You got lots of strokes for playing by the rules, so you rolled along as the good girl, always eager to please your parents, your teachers, your bosses."

She stopped at the top of the stairs. "Are you trying to tell me I'm *not* a good girl?"

He eased her coat off her shoulders and hung it on the coatrack. "Like Mae West once said . . . when you're good, you're very good, but when you're bad . . . you're better."

"I think Mae West was referring to her sexual talents."

Pete grinned, moving in on her like a jungle cat going after something unsuspecting and tasty. "That too."

She took a step backward, but his hands had already freed her blouse from her skirt. "Hey!"

"We don't need you to be wired anymore. No sense wasting the battery." He'd worn his share of listening devices and knew the best way to remove them was in one fell swope. He grabbed an end of the surgical tape and yanked.

"Yeow!"

"Sorry about that." His fingers skimmed over the stinging flesh, soothing and arousing. "Feel better?"

She could only blink at him.

He unhooked her bra and caught the transmitter as it fell out. With his other hand he cupped a breast, passing his thumb over the already hardening tip, thinking clandestine operations were a lot more fun with Louisa as a partner.

She was paralyzed. A wild animal caught in the beam of a searchlight, held captive as his fingers continued to excite. He watched as he teased, fascinated by the power he held over her, by his ability to give pleasure, knowing he was as much the enslaved as the enslaver.

Louisa could barely breathe for the sensations pulsing through her body. He knew all her secret pleasures. He knew how and where to touch and kiss. And he knew the words she liked to hear . . . words of endearment, words of passion.

He rummaged through the freezer and pulled out a bag of homemade raviolis he'd gotten from the Italian deli on Connecticut. He set a pot of water to boil and scrounged a box of crushed, sun-dried tomatoes from the over-the-counter cupboard.

"You're really very domestic," Louisa said. She was at the table, wearing his big terry robe, feeling very lazy. She was resigned to the fact that she had no willpower when it came to the sexual attraction between them and had reached the conclusion that it wouldn't hurt to enjoy it.

He looked around the apartment and laughed out loud. She was right. He'd become domestic. If someone had said that to him ten years earlier, he'd have broken his nose. "I used to live like Kurt."

"What happened?"

"You know how some people find religion late in life? I found middle class." He threw a frozen ravioli in Spike's direction, and the cat attacked it.

Louisa didn't want to burst his bubble, but he wasn't exactly middle-class. She was on intimate terms with middle-class and knew for a fact that owning a luxury sports car and a three-thousand-dollar tux was *not* typical middle-class. She supposed he meant he'd found middle-class values, but she wasn't so sure of that, either. The men in her parents' neighborhood didn't wear pony-tails, and didn't hang out with wire-tappers. She amended that last part to *illegal* wiretappers. After all, it was Washington.

He dropped a handful of ice cubes into a goblet, poured cola over it, and gave the drink to Louisa. He was still feeling the aftershocks of their lovemaking—violent ripples of affection that grabbed him in the gut and sent panicky messages of love and commitment to his brain. He wasn't ready to deal with messages of com-mitment, so he got himself a cold beer and took a long pull on the bottle. "Tell me more about being different."

She tried for casual reserve but had no luck. The excitement bubbled out at the first oppor-tunity to discuss her new plans. "I want to return to school. I want to be a lawyer."

It caught him by surprise. He hadn't expected a career change, but now that he thought about it, it made sense. He'd gone through a similar metamorphosis. He ran it through his mind one more time and nodded. "You'd make a terrific lawyer."

"You really think so?"

"Yup. I think you should go for it."

She'd badly wanted someone to say it, to encourage her. She flashed him a brilliant smile and felt her eyes mist over for a split second. She lowered her lashes and sipped her drink, embar-rassed that she'd almost burst into tears at the thought of becoming a lawyer. It was amazing how such a powerful dream could be buried so deep that it had been all but forgotten.

He saw the joy and the emotion and had a hard time not crying along with her. He gave himself a fast lecture on macho behavior, took a hard breath, and steadied his voice. "Okay, so it's settled," he said. "You're going to be a lawyer. What else is different?"

"I'm more assertive." She shook her finger at him. "Don't try to push me around. I won't stand for it."

He pretended to be offended.

Louisa ignored him. "I want to be treated like an equal in this pig project."

"You want to be an equal to Kurt? Honey, even I don't want to be an equal to Kurt."

"You know what I mean."

He knew exactly what she meant. She didn't want him being overprotective of her. It was an unreasonable demand. He could more easily stop breathing than stop wanting to keep her safe. "I understand your point of view," he said. "From now on you're one of the boys." It was an outright lie, and he didn't feel the least bit guilty about making it. There was more to love than truth, he told himself. There was survival.

Eight

Louisa didn't like working for Stu Maislin. The atmosphere in his suite of offices was oppressive, his administrative assistant looked like a bookie, and she suspected her phone was bugged by both Kurt and Maislin. It was like living in a goldfish bowl filled with piranha.

She was on her third day on the job, and she was still wearing a wire at Pete's insistence. He was outside, somewhere, listening to her every word. To say she had no secrets was an understatement. "I wonder if I unplugged the iron?" she said into her chest. "Hope it doesn't burn the house down. And did you remember to close the front door after you went back in for my briefcase? I bet the house isn't locked up." She smiled, knowing she drove Pete crazy with these mutterings. It was the only fun part of her workday. "Only kidding," she said. "I'm pretty sure I unplugged the iron. I don't think it would burst into flames, anyway, because I had it on a low setting because I was ironing my red silk teddy. You remember that teddy? The one I wore the night before last? The one with the wide, easy-lovin' legs? I wore that teddy to the office today because I thought I might take an extra long lunch hour and"—she crinkled a paper, simulating static—"and when I was done with you, you'd be sitting funny for the rest of the afternoon."

She allowed herself another smile and turned to the stack of mail on her desk, thinking he now had something to occupy his mind while she did some work. She was halfway through the mail when a check slipped through her fingers. It had been delivered earlier by a bonded messenger. Not an unusual occurrence. She'd signed for it and placed it in the priority bin. It was to Maislin, personally. And it was against a claim on his homeowner's insurance, to the tune of slightly less than half a million. She did a silent whistle. It was a lot of money, and it pricked her curiosity. She copied the claim number, the amount, the name of the adjuster and his phone number, and went down the hall to the public phone. She dialed the adjuster and introduced herself. She was new, she explained. She needed to be brought up to speed on Mr. Maislin's claim.

Pete was at the water fountain behind her when she hung up. "Well?" he asked.

"Couldn't wait until I got off work?"

"I was intrigued."

"Maislin's house was broken into five days before the pig incident. A very expensive pair of diamond earrings, a choker, and two rings were stolen. The thief also took several stamps which were extremely valuable. They were insured for big bucks."

"Never found?"

"Never found," Louisa said.

"You think the pig could have eaten them?"

She wrinkled her nose.

"I'm serious. Years ago, before Reuters sent me to Central America, I did an article on insurance fraud. It's common. If you're a big roller and times get tough, you fake a burglary. That way you get paid twice. You collect the insurance, and then you turn around and you sell the family jewels under the table. Suppose Maislin needed money. Suppose he had Bucky steal the stuff and Bucky was supposed to feed it to Petunia. Petunia was being shipped to Amsterdam. Maybe there was a contact in Amsterdam, waiting to fence the jewelry and stamps."

"The pig wouldn't have any problem with customs."

"Exactly."

"Sounds pretty farfetched. How were they supposed to get the jewelry and stamps out of the pig."

"That's the beauty of the plan," Pete said. "The jewelry and stamps would come out all by themselves. In one end, out the other."

"Ugh."

"It would have been brilliant if the pig hadn't wandered off."

"So now they're going to try it again," Louisa said.

"Precisely, Watson."

"I don't want to be Watson. Watson was fat and dopey. I want to be Holmes. You can be Watson."

"You're never satisfied."

"This is my new assertive personality," she said.

"Maybe we could take turns being assertive. You can be assertive on Monday, Wednesday, Friday and alternate Saturdays. I can be assertive on Tuesday, Thursday, and Sunday."

"It's worth considering. I suppose I need to get back to work and keep my ear to the ground. We don't want to miss any of this swiney intrigue."

Pete watched her return to Maislin's office. Now that the mystery might be solved, he wasn't sure he wanted to continue. There were worse things in the world than insurance fraud. It was white-collar crime, and no one would be surprised to find Maislin guilty of such a thing. In fact, people sort of expected it of him. It was almost his most outstanding job skill. Rationalization, Pete admitted. It all came back to Louisa. He didn't want her involved in a sting operation. Was he willing to let Maislin off the hook to keep Louisa safe? Yes. He was a rotten patriot, but there it was. Louisa was his first priority. Not that it mattered. She'd sunk her teeth into this, and he didn't think she was going to let go.

They stopped by Kurt's apartment on the way home from work. They brought a pizza—double cheese with the works—and a six-pack of beer. They filled Kurt in on the insurance claim.

"Hard to believe Maislin needs money," Louisa said. "He has a big house, expensive cars and clothes, an extensive portfolio. He's a millionaire several times over."

"On paper," Pete said. "I checked into him. He has serious cash-flow problems."

Kurt chugged a beer. "And an even more serious drug problem. I've been picking it up on the tap. He doesn't get all that aggressive energy from eating a balanced diet. The man runs on nose candy and rock." He looked over at Louisa. "That's cocaine and crack."

"I know what it is. Are you sure?"

Kurt nodded. "He's made two buys this week alone."

Louisa felt sick. She might be a little jaded when it came to glorifying a senator or a congressman, but she believed in the American political system. She'd been on the Hill long enough to know the vast majority of the elected officials took their responsibility seriously and worked long and hard. Sometimes a man got carried away with his own importance or succumbed to the pressure of the job, and a scandal ensued. She was always sad to see that happen.

In this case, there was little sadness for Maislin. She'd had a chance to observe him firsthand and had come to thoroughly dislike him and distrust him.

Pete saw the color leave her face. He covered her hand with his. "You okay?"

"No, I'm *not* okay. I'm furious. How could he betray the voters like this? How could he be so stupid? So arrogantly corrupt as to put himself above the law?"

Pete grinned. "She's going to be a lawyer someday," he said to Kurt. "She's going to be dynamite."

"A lawyer?" Kurt said. "No kidding? Hey, that's terrific."

Louisa blushed. "It's actually only in the planning stage. I haven't even taken my LSATs."

"Don't worry about the LSATs. Pete and me'll help you study. And if that doesn't work, I can get into their computer. I can give you any grade you want."

She was touched. She was also horrified, but she told herself Kurt's intentions were good. Maybe Kurt wasn't such a bad guy. Just a tad misdirected. She took another look at him. Who was she kidding? He might have a good heart, but his brain had mental deviant engraved on the frontal lobes. Kurt was frighteningly weird.

Pete watched the play of emotions on Louisa's face and could hardly keep from laughing out loud. He knew exactly what she was thinking. He'd gone through the same thought process many times himself and had always reached the same conclusion about Kurt. In Central America he'd worked with entire units of Kurt types—bottom-line personalities. The end always justifies the means. It was a convenient philosophy to take into combat.

Louisa slid another tray of chocolate chip cookies into the oven and set the timer. At four-thirty in the afternoon the sky was gunmetal gray and the outside air cold enough to make her kitchen window frost. Inside, the house was filled with the warm smell of freshly baked cookies and melted chocolate.

Louisa leaned against the counter and wondered why she was feeling so cranky. It was Saturday. She had the whole day to herself. She had her life under control. She had exciting plans for the future. She'd gotten her way with the pig project. She was sexually satisfied. Why wasn't she happy?

She looked up at the ceiling. The source of all discontent, she thought. She was in love with Pete Streeter, and she didn't like it. He was all wrong for her. In fact, he was probably all wrong for *anybody*. And she loved him. She rolled her eyes and flapped her arms. Love was stupid. It made no sense. After so many years of being so careful, she'd gone and fallen in love with Pete Streeter. Go figure.

She nibbled on a warm cookie. She was going to ignore the "L" word, of course. She absolutely was *not* going to say it out loud, and she especially wasn't going to say it out loud to Pete. She was certain this was a temporary condition. All she had to do was wait it out.

Pete could smell the cookies baking downstairs in Louisa's oven. She was torturing him, he thought. She knew he had to work, and since early morning she'd been producing the most distracting sounds and smells . . . sighs and stretches, rustles of clothing, snatches of tunes hummed between chores, and now the cookies. He looked at the computer screen in front of him and swore out loud. He was doing rewrites and sending them to the coast by modem, because he didn't want to leave Louisa. Ordinarily, he'd be in L.A. by now, gearing up to go on location. In a few days they were going to start shooting, and he was going to have to be on call for daily page changes. It wasn't the sort of thing he felt comfortable doing long distance.

Unfortunately, Louisa refused to give up the pig investigation. They'd tapped Maislin's home phone and tagged his car with a transmitter. They'd alerted the insurance company and were working with a fraud investigator. In his opinion, Louisa was superfluous. The insurance investigator didn't share that opinion. And Louisa wasn't budging from her desk until Maislin was caught with the goods.

So here he was, torn between his work and Louisa Brannigan. It was frustrating, especially since he didn't know *why* he was in this predicament. It wasn't as if she needed him. Once she'd gotten it into her mind to take control of her life, she'd done it with a vengeance. He was the one who'd told her to cut the umbilical; now he felt like Dr. Frankenstein.

He saved his file, stood, and stretched. He was meeting her parents later that night. She'd been invited home to dinner, and she was dragging him along. He suspected it was one last vestige of cowardice, but he didn't care. He was curious about the typical suburban family. As a kid he'd desperately wanted to be adopted by Donna Reed, as a teenager he'd struck out against the saccharine unreality of the heartland image, and as an adult he wondered if the coveted clean, harmonious, upper-middle-class, Cape-Cod-house, dog-sleeping-on-the-hearth family actually existed.

Two hours later he found himself shaking his head in disbelief. There it was in front of him—a white brick Cape Cod with black shutters, a white picket fence, and a flagstone front walk. Even in winter it was nicely landscaped with lots of big holly and azalea bushes bordered with silver-dollar wood chip mulch. It had a brick chimney, which he was sure led to a living room fireplace and had been designed with Santa Claus in mind. No disrespect intended—he really was very impressed.

The door flew open before they had a chance to knock, and the frame was filled with Louisa's father, dressed in a knit shirt and sans-a-belt pants. "Mike Brannigan," he said to Pete. "Good to meet you." The man was medium height and stocky, his complexion was ruddy, his outstretched hand was short fingered and meaty. He was a Brannigan through and through.

Pete saw the man's eyes take in the ponytail, but the hand didn't weaken and the welcoming smile didn't fade. He gave him a few points for that.

Louisa's mother was close behind her husband. "Kathy Brannigan," she said, extending her hand. Her hair was short and feathered with gray, her face was friendly. She was wearing gray University of Maryland sweats and red high-top basketball shoes. "You'll have to excuse the way I look," she said. "I just got back from the library."

Louisa shook her head. "June Cleaver never dressed like that."

"Who?"

"June Cleaver. Beaver's mother."

Kathy Brannigan gave her daughter a wan smile. "When you were five and Susan Fielding's mother knitted her a ski hat, I took up knitting. When you were seven and Carolyn Chenko's mother made homemade bread, I gave baking bread a shot. I decorated cakes better than Amy Butcher's mother, went on more field trips than Jennifer O'Neil's mother, and baked better chocolate chip cookies than any mother in the history of the world. I draw the line at dressing like June Cleaver."

"Mom's gone back to college," Louisa explained to Pete. "She's a sophomore."

"I missed it the first time around," Kathy said. "I was busy doing the mother thing."

Pete handed over his jacket and checked the hearth for a sleeping dog. He wasn't disappointed. The furniture was dark wood and freshly polished. The couch was overstuffed and homey. The house smelled like woodsmoke and apple pie. He wouldn't have believed any of this if he hadn't seen it firsthand, he thought.

Louisa's mother tapped Pete on the arm. "Are you all right? Your eyes look a little glazed."

"It's the pie fumes," he said.

She led him into the living room and seated him in a wingback. "Don't get too choked up over it. It's one of those frozen ones that you just put in the oven and bake."

He didn't care. A pie was a pie.

Mike brought him a beer and set a basket of chips at his elbow. "I hear you're one of those Hollywood types."

"I write screenplays."

"You know Burt Lancaster?"

"Uh, no."

Louisa caught a glimpse of the dining room table. It was set for five. She looked at her mother and the question silently passed between them.

"Grandma Brannigan," Louisa's mother said. "She's visiting for a few days."

"Oh boy."

"I heard that," Grandma Brannigan called

from the kitchen. "You always did have a smart mouth."

Everyone in the living room exchanged looks of suffering."

"She's really very sweet," Louisa's mother whispered.

"I heard that too," Grandma Brannigan yelled. "And God's gonna get you for lying, Katherine." She shuffled into the living room. She was a forbidding chunk of a woman with a square Irish face and a square Irish body. She had an apron over her gray wool skirt and white blouse, and she held a wooden spoon in her hand as if it were a weapon. "I'm not sweet at all," she said to Pete. "Who are you?"

He rose and offered his hand. "Pete Streeter. I'm Louisa's friend."

She took his hand and squinted at him. "You look silly with that pony tail."

He turned to Louisa. "Help."

"Are you crazy?" Louisa said. "I can barely hold my own with her. Don't look for help here."

"So," Grandma Brannigan said, "are you sleeping with my granddaughter?"

"Uh, well . . ."

Everyone sat up a little straighter and leaned forward ever so slightly, waiting for his reply.

He eyeballed the spoon in her hand. "You gonna hit me with that if I say yes?"

"I might hit you with it, anyway, just on general principle."

"Well hell," Pete said, "then I might as well deserve it."

Louisa was on her feet, pulling him into the dining room. "Time to eat."

Pete smiled lazily. "Thought you weren't coming to my rescue?"

"You were going to hang me out to dry!"

He smiled and shrugged, and Louisa kicked him hard in the ankle.

He squelched a shriek of pain into a grunt.

"I get my violent nature from Grandma Brannigan," Louisa said.

"Maybe I'll take you home to Hellertown for Easter. You'll fit right in. You can sucker punch my sister-in-law for first dibs on the potato salad."

"Gee, I'm really looking forward to it."

Pete slung an arm around her and hugged her to him. "I bet you got smacked a lot with that wooden spoon."

"Not once. She's all bristly on the outside and soft as marshmallow on the inside."

"That's a terrible thing to say about a person," her grandmother said. "And it's a bald-faced lie. I'm hard as nails on the inside. Don't you believe a word she tells you," she said to Pete. "It's from the Krueger side of the family." She slid a glance at Louisa's mother and lowered her voice. "The Kruegers always had a time with the truth, if you know what I mean."

He could hear Louisa's mother sigh behind him, and it sent a smile twitching at the corners of his mouth. He liked this family. *Really* liked them. They were a little looney and a little exasperated with one another. They were his kind of people.

"Cripes," Louisa's father said. "Lay off the Kruegers, will you, Ma?"

"Everybody knows . . ."

Louisa's mother brought a platter of fried chicken to the table.

"Look at this," Grandma Brannigan said, "she had this delivered. Can you imagine? A dinner party that comes from a cardboard bucket. Biscuits, coleslaw, everything."

"I have an exam on Monday," Louisa's mother said. "I didn't have time to cook."

"You could have asked me," Grandma said. "I would have made a roast."

"I asked you. You said we should order chicken."

"Lies. All lies."

Everyone sighed together.

Pete loved it. It was just as he'd always imagined. He took a piece of chicken and two biscuits and wondered if it was too late to get adopted.

Louisa picked at her skirt in the dark car, on the way home. "Sorry I kicked you so hard. I got carried away."

"It wasn't that hard. It just caught me by surprise. You can make up for it when we get home."

"You have something specific in mind?"

"Did I ever tell you I have a video camera?"

"No!"

"Yes."

"Oh dear." She giggled.

On Sunday it rained and Louisa felt caged. She paced in Pete's apartment while he typed at the computer. Kurt had been over earlier with tapes from Maislin's home phone. Maislin had called Bucky and given him a date. Tuesday. She cracked her knuckles and cleared her throat. She was nervous. They didn't have enough information. If more information wasn't forthcoming over the phone lines by the next afternoon, it was going to be up to her to get it. She splayed her hands on the cool windowpane and stared out at the wet road. She was in over her head, and there was no turning back.

Pete saw the apprehension in the set of her shoulders. Finally, she was scared. Good. Fear would make her careful. He looked at the printed words on the screen and then at the woman huddled at the window. He had hours more work, but he couldn't concentrate. He swore to himself and saved his file."You got a raincoat?" he called.

"What'd you have in mind?"

He took her hand and pulled her from the window. "The zoo."

They walked the distance. They wore slickers and rain hats and were dripping wet and half frozen by the time they got to the entrance. They pressed on, through the big iron gates, up the wide cement pathway. They headed for the elephant trail. They didn't talk. They barely looked at the habitats. They kept their heads down against the rain and the wind until they reached the cavernous building that housed the giraffes and hippos. They blew through the doors and stopped short, almost knocked over by the steamy heat and rich scent of animal hide and dung. They shook off the rain and stared at each other with purple lips and chattering teeth.

"I love Washington weather," Pete said. "It makes you so miserable, you forget all your other problems."

Louisa nodded and stomped her feet, trying to get some feeling back. "Puts things in perspective." She looked up at him, a little shocked. "Do you have problems?"

He blinked once, very slowly. "You. You're my problem."

It wasn't a surprise. She'd seen him trying to sandwich his work into days that were spent baby-sitting her. And she knew there was more. He was undoubtedly caught in the same emotional turmoil she'd been fighting. There was an incredibly strong attraction between them that had no basis in good sense. "Hmm," she said, because she didn't have a decent answer.

They watched the giraffe eat, watched the elephants get hosed down. They stared at the hippos half submerged in tepid water. Then they put their hats on, zipped their slickers, and went back outside. They ran most of the way home, splashing through puddles in their haste, soaking their jeans from the knees down. They were breathless when they reached home. They stripped at the top of the stairs, fell into Pete's bed, and made love like there was no tomorrow. When they were done, they sat at the kitchen table and ate hot dogs and baked beans and a half gallon of coffee ice cream.

"So, you think I'm a problem, huh?" Louisa asked.

He knew she'd get back to it. "You're a problem with no apparent solution. No matter what I do about you, it's wrong."

She could read between the lines. She felt the same way. That didn't mean she liked it. Being a problem wasn't exactly flattering. It was one thing for *him* to be a problem. That was understandable. *He* was far from perfect. She, on the other hand, was much closer. Yeah, right. She did some mental eye rolling, and thought the ugly truth was they probably deserved each other.

She felt the nagging crankiness beginning to return, and she pushed it away with a change of topic. She moved the conversation to the one area they had in common—the pig. "There's something I don't understand about this pig thing," she said. "What happened to the first pig? We know it got sick and wandered away. We know Maislin still has the jewelry. We know they didn't want you asking questions. So, what happened to the pig?"

"Probably Bucky found it and was able to

sneak it out of the Hart Building. My guess is he's got his freezer filled with pork chops."

"Are you going to make this into a screenplay?"

He shook his head. "Nobody'd believe it . . . and there's not enough violence."

Nine

Louisa cracked her knuckles and pressed her hand against her breastbone, checking on the hidden transmitter for the thirtieth time in the past two hours. Maislin had been in a committee hearing all morning but was expected into his office shortly. She was supposed to plant a bug on Maislin when he walked through the door. The moment of truth, she thought grimly. The listening device Kurt had given her was a black piece of plastic, half the size of a matchbook. It was voice activated, would last for six hours of operation, and cost seven hundred dollars. Louisa expected it was also illegal. No one had mentioned that aspect of it. There were some things best left unsaid.

She jumped in her seat when Maislin stormed through the door, and her heart turned over with a sickening thud when she saw his mood.

As was often the case, Stu Maislin was not joyous. He had no tolerance for colleagues who disagreed with him, and several had done just that in his committee meeting. His cheeks were scarlet from the exertion of controlling his temper, and his jowls shook as he pounded past Louisa's desk. At close range, Maislin had the presence of an army tank at full idle. Louisa could practically feel the floor shaking under him.

He stopped at the entrance to his inner office to review his day's itinerary with the administrative assistant, and Louisa rushed to her feet. She knew what she had to do. Kurt had rehearsed with her. She knew about physical contact and diversionary tactics. She knew about positioning herself so the rest of the office staff couldn't see the plant being made.

Her heart rose to her throat, and her pulse pounded in her ears. This sort of thing looked so much easier on television, she thought. And it had sounded so simple when Kurt had suggested it. Now that she was on her feet she felt frozen in time, her shoes rooted to the floor. If she didn't hurry, she'd miss her opportunity.

She closed her eyes and swallowed hard. She was sure Eddie Murphy never had problems like this. She was sure his feet always took him where he wanted to go. That's the difference between me and Eddie Murphy, she thought. I have Chevy Chase feet, and Eddie Murphy has Eddie Murphy feet. Why hadn't she realized that when they were making these ridiculous plans?

She looked down at her legs and silently ordered them to do something . . . anything! Miraculously, they took her across the room to within inches of Maislin. She pretended to stumble, and crashed smack into him with a lot more impact than she'd intended. "Oops," she said on a whoosh of expelled air. She clutched at his jacket for support and attempted to drop the bug into his pocket, but her hands were sweating and shaking, and the bug slid short and rolled onto the floor. Louisa saw her whole life flash in front of her eyes.

Maislin swore under his breath and grabbed Louisa by the arm, his thumb brushing against her breast in the process. He prolonged the contact and brought her up close to his face. "You want to do the two-step, we can go into my inner office where we'll have more privacy," he said.

Louisa caught a glimpse of the bug sitting black and malevolent on the floor. No one had noticed it fall. She blinked at Maislin with big innocent eyes. "I slipped."

The thumb did a fast exploratory. "Maybe you should slip more often."

Louisa wrenched herself away. "Maybe you should eat dirt and die."

Maislin narrowed his eyes at her. "What?"

"Listen, you miserable scumbag, you try that again, and I'll make sure you're in a lot of pain. You understand?"

Maislin just glared at her, and she glared back, thinking anger did wonderful things for her personality. Eddie Murphy eat your heart out.

"I'll deal with you later," Maislin finally said. He wheeled around and stormed off to his office.

Louisa bent to retrieve the bug. She took it back to her desk and sat quietly, waiting to stop shaking, staring down at the odious piece of black plastic. Now what? Now she was going to have to find another way to insert the blasted thing in his pocket. She was going to have to crawl back into his office with her tail between her legs and ooze up next to him. Not an appealing thought.

Pete was parked half a block away in the Porsche, listening. "Damn," he said. "What'd he do? *What'd he do?*" He wrapped his fingers around the steering wheel and counted to ten. Then he counted to ten again. He hated this. He hated sitting in the Porsche, feeling impotent. Hellertown might have its faults, but men grew up knowing their responsibilities. Roles were clear. Men didn't sit around, listening to their women take abuse from other men, and disputes were settled with good old-fashioned physical violence. Man to man. It didn't feel right that Louisa should be in there taking all the risks, threatening to hurt Maislin. Hurting Maislin should be his job, Pete thought. Instead, he was stuck in his car with a radio strapped to his head. He slumped in his seat, thinking he would have been happier in the nineteenth century. This man/woman business was just too complicated now.

Louisa took a deep breath and smoothed the wrinkles from her skirt. She picked some lint from her blouse and checked to see if her nail polish was cracked. She was procrastinating. She didn't want to confront Maislin again. "All right, already," she said into her chest. "Don't worry. I'll do it. I'll do it."

Pete sat up straighter. "What? What?" he shouted.

She took the day's mail from her desk and headed for Maislin. The mail was a legitimate excuse, she told herself. Nothing demeaning or extraordinary about delivering the mail. She squared her shoulders, knocked twice, and entered the office. Maislin was on the phone, with his back to her. His jacket was slung over a chair by the door! "Mail," Louisa said, weak with relief at her good fortune. She flipped the bug into his suit jacket pocket on the way out and closed the door behind her. "Mission accomplished."

Pete lunged out of the car and strode across the street to the Hart Building. There was a limo at curbside. Maislin's limo, he thought. He stood, waiting for close to a half hour, with his fists balled in the pockets of his shearling jacket. At last, Maislin swept through the doors with several aides in tow and plunged into the plush interior of the limo.

Pete felt the rage centering in his chest, felt his fist itching to pop Maislin one in the nose. Patience, he told himself. Hold out for long-term satisfaction—go for a congressional investigation, criminal charges, a drug bust.

He watched the limo pull away and slowly move down the street. Then he watched Kurt move after him in a late-model midsize Ford. Pete had ridden in the car many times. It had a custom V-8 engine under the hood, and hidden under the dash was a CB, a flush-mounted tracker with a dropped display panel, and a very large gun. Stashed under the backseat were more tools of his trade, and it was anybody's guess what was in the trunk. His trunk could hold anything from hot watches to dead bodies to Stinger missiles.

Pete rubbernecked at the steady stream of secretaries and aides on lunch errands trickling out of the building, then he plastered a smile on his face and went after Louisa.

She was alone in the office when Pete ambled up to her desk. He had his thumbs hooked into his jeans' pockets so that his open jacket revealed a black T-shirt stretched across smooth chest muscles and a rock-hard, washboard stomach. The washed-out jeans hugged tight hips and held the telltale contour of a man who wore bikini briefs. He had his hair pulled back and his full mouth was curved into a lazy smile. His eyes were shaded and filled with sexual promise. And under the facade, he fairly vibrated with suppressed violence.

The quintessential male, Louisa thought. Gorgeous . . . but not totally evolved. "You look as if you're about to rupture something," she said.

He expelled a long breath and kicked Louisa's desk, hard.

"Feel better?"

He had to think about it a minute. "No." He opened her bottom drawer and removed her purse. "Let's get out of here."

"I have work to do."

"You're done working for this creep." He wanted to take her home and make love to her. He wanted to go to bed and stay there until he felt at peace. No pigs. No politicians. Just Louisa and him locked away from the world for a little while.

For days he'd listened to her heartbeat come through the headset. He was no longer wearing the headset, but he still felt the soft thrum of her pulse. He would always feel it, he thought, the way a child in utero feels the tattoo of his mother's heart and probably always remembers it somewhere deep in his subconscious. There was a word for it . . . bonding. He was bonded to Louisa. The thought hit him like a fist in the gut, and suddenly everything fell into place. He loved her. He would always love her. His love was deep and real and comforting. For the first time in his life, he didn't feel panic-stricken at the thought of marriage and commitment. He smiled at Louisa and kissed her on the nose.

She looked at him warily. "What's that smile all about?"

"We need to talk."

Louisa changed into jeans and a rugby shirt and made her way up the stairs to Pete's apartment. He was making cream of tomato soup and grilled cheese sandwiches, and Spike was prowling the area around the stove in anticipation.

"Okay," Louisa said, pouring two mugs of soup, and taking her place at the table. "What do you want to talk about?"

Pete handed out the grilled cheese. "Marriage."

Louisa felt her stomach dip. She looked up from her soup. "Marriage?"

"Yep. I think we should get married."

She put her spoon down and squinted at him. "Are you feeling all right?"

"Never felt better."

"Marriage," she repeated. "To each other?"

"It came to me while I was standing at your desk."

"I thought we'd decided we were incompatible."

"There's all kinds of incompatibility. It seems to me our incompatibility isn't nearly so incompatible as some other kinds of incompatibility."

"Gee, that makes me feel a lot better."

It was too fast, he realized. She hadn't been hit by the bonding revelation the way he had. And she didn't know how short their time was together. He had a studio breathing down his neck. It wouldn't be many more days before he received an ultimatum to get his butt out to the coast. "I should have gotten a ring first," he said. "I should have done something romantic."

"That part doesn't bother me."

"What then?"

"Eternity. I'm bothered by eternity. You know, 'til death do us part?"

"Do you love me?"

She stirred her soup. "That's not the point."

"Aha! So, you admit to it! You *do* love me!"

"Just because you love someone doesn't mean you have to marry him."

"No, but it makes things a lot easier. Besides, I'm a real catch. I'm relatively good looking, I'm great in bed, I'm rich, I'm fun at the zoo . . ."

"What about my independence? You know, charting my own course, running my own life."

"I don't want to take away your independence. I want to share in it."

"That's what my mother said when she persuaded me to go to the University of Maryland as a commuter."

"There are alternatives to marriage. We could get engaged and live together in sin. That sounds like fun, doesn't it?"

"I'm going to tell Grandma Brannigan you said that."

He dredged up a smile, reached across the table, and covered her hand with his. "Think about it."

Kurt showed up on Pete's doorstep at five-thirty. He had tapes stuffed into his ski-jacket pocket and his fingers hooked into a six-pack of beer. He set the beer on the counter, peeled one out of the cardboard container, and popped the top. "You did good," he said to Louisa. "Between the car phone and the bug in Maislin's coat, I was able to get everything I needed. Not only did I find out the pig's flight, but Maislin and Bucky had a nice conversation about how the insurance company deserved to get hit." He flipped the tapes to Pete. "These are yours. You paid for them, you get to keep them. There's even a bonus tape dedicated to his drug buys."

"What about the insurance company and the police?" Louisa asked. "Don't they want the tapes?"

"Can't use them," Pete said. "We bypassed a few technicalities."

"Then what are you going to do with them?"

Pete grinned. "Give them to the media . . . anonymously."

"That should end his political career."

"Yeah, and when the animal rights activists get through with him, he'll be nothing more than a grease spot on the pavement," Kurt said. He had his head in Pete's refrigerator. He came out with a plastic container of leftover hot dogs and beans and went in search of a fork. "There's a loose end I need to tie up. I need to get the bug back. It's still in Maislin's pocket. If he found it, he might get nervous and call the deal off. Besides, it has Louisa's prints on it." He saw the look on Pete's face and held up a hand. "No problem. He's on ice at a benefit dinner. In about an hour and a half he'll be full of chicken almondine and his own self-importance. All I need to know is which pocket."

"The left," Louisa said. "Suit jacket."

"They're not going to let you close to him dressed like that," Pete said. "You're too scruffy looking."

Kurt tossed the empty plastic container in the sink. "That's why I'm here. I need a clean shirt."

By the time he was ready to rendezvous with Maislin, he had more than a clean shirt. He had a suit, topcoat, shirt, shoes, and tie.

"Where's the dinner?" Pete asked.

"The French embassy."

Pete handed him the keys to the Porsche. "This'll help you get through the gate."

Kurt grinned. "I hope I don't see anybody I know. This is gonna shoot my image all to hell."

Louisa watched Kurt disappear down the stairs, heard the front door slam behind him. "He actually looked human."

"An illusion," Pete said.

They were playing Monopoly when Kurt returned. He helped himself to another beer and headed for the bedroom. Five minutes later he emerged in his own clothes.

Pete rolled the dice. "Any problems?"

"None."

"Want to play?"

Kurt snorted. "Pass."

"I listened to the tapes. They're pretty condemning."

"Amateurs," Kurt said. "They even call each other by name. You'd think people would have learned from Watergate."

"You going to be in on the kill tomorrow?"

"I might listen from a discreet distance."

"Thanks for helping out," Pete said.

"You'll get my bill."

Louisa shifted next to Pete, enjoying the slide of skin over skin. The room was velvety dark and comfortably warm. They were loosely entwined in a tangle of sheets. Louisa looked at the bright blue digital numbers on Pete's beside clock. It was almost five A.M. They'd spent the better part of the night making love, talking about childhoods, sharing secrets. She turned to the man next to her and dropped a gentle kiss on his bare shoulder. He sighed and smiled, reflexively drawing her closer, but he didn't wake up. She watched him in the darkened room, fascinated by her own love for him, silently wondering about his marriage proposal. It had caught her off guard, and she was afraid she hadn't responded tactfully.

She eased away, dressed herself in one of his T-shirts, and padded to the front window. She wanted to see the sunrise. She wanted to sit in the dark, waiting for the sky to lighten, and she wanted to think about all the new beginnings in her life. And she supposed she should think about marriage. Could she spend the rest of her life with a scriptwriter who was movie-star handsome and only recently domesticated? He'd always have a little bit of the chauvinist hustler in him. And she'd always blithely ignore it. Once the honeymoon was over, they'd drive each other nuts. She shook her head. This wasn't exactly a match made in heaven.

Pete felt her leave his side, and the loss was enough to bring him awake. He watched her drop the T-shirt over her head and silently move to the window. He thought she looked like a tousled ghost. A sliver of cheek hung pale and tempting beneath the shirt. It was an enchanting sight, but he was sexually exhausted. It had taken hours of hard work for him to reach this state, so he felt there was no shame in his contentment. He rolled onto his stomach and closed his eyes.

Three hours later he woke to the smell of blueberry muffins and coffee. He dressed in his favorite ratty old sweats and padded out to the kitchen. He slid his arms around Louisa and kissed the back of her neck. "You're up early this morning."

"Couldn't sleep."

"Wondering about the pig?"

"Among other things." She poured two cups of coffee. "Bucky was supposed to put pig number two on a seven-thirty flight. I sort of wish I'd been there. I feel left out."

The phone rang and they both jumped, knowing it would be Kurt. Pete took the call. When he hung up, he was smiling. "The pig was stuffed with the jewelry, all right. The metal parts showed up in the X ray. And when they confronted Bucky, he squealed louder than the pig."

"I suppose that means I'm out of a job," Louisa said.

"That's okay. You need to get busy on those law school applications, anyway." He sunk his teeth into a muffin and reached for the paper. "See, this is what married life is all about. After a night of outstanding sex, the wife gets up early, bakes muffins, gets the paper from the front porch, and makes fresh coffee."

"If you're trying to talk me into getting married, you're failing miserably."

"What does a woman want out of a marriage?"

"Undying devotion and a warm place to put her cold feet when she gets into bed at night."

"You could get that from a golden retriever."

"Exactly." Louisa finished her coffee and put the cup in the dishwasher. "I have to go. I have to clean out my desk. Maislin won't be in until this afternoon, and I'd just as soon have the job done before he shows up."

"You want company?"

She kissed him on the top of the head. "No, but thanks for offering. There isn't a whole lot to do. I need to type out a formal letter of resignation, reclaim some personal belongings, and file a sexual harassment complaint."

"Go for it," he said.

"How about I bring some Chinese food home with me for supper."

"I like the hot stuff with the peanuts in it."

It was gray and drizzling when Louisa straggled out of the subway entrance. She ran across the street to Wuc Don's Chinese Restaurant and pushed through the double-door entrance. Heat poured from an overhead vent, and dishes clattered in the kitchen. It was a small, hole-in-the-wall restaurant that did seventy percent of its trade in take-out. The woodwork was black lacquer, the wallpaper was red flocked, the lighting was dim enough to hide the stains on the red-and-gold carpet. Louisa ordered four different dishes plus rice and fried noodles.

Fifteen minutes later she trudged up Connecticut with her bags and white cardboard cartons. She'd stayed away all afternoon, wandering around museums, trying to come to terms with her feelings about marriage. She'd almost reached the conclusion that it might not be so bad, when a mental image of her wedding had flashed into her brain.

The wedding was being held in her parents' house, and she was in a trim white suit with her mother's pearls at her neck. She walked down the stairs on her father's arm, then together they walked through the small cluster of guests assembled in the living room. Her grandmother Brannigan was to one side, dressed in black, fingering her rosary, mouth set, eyes narrow. "You'll rot in hell for not being married in a church," she said.

"There was no time," Louisa tried to explain. "Besides, I haven't been to church in seven years."

Even now, as Louisa turned the corner, she could feel herself break out into a cold sweat of Catholic guilt.

The vision of the wedding continued. Louisa saw herself nod and smile at Mr. and Mrs. Szalagy. "You look absolutely lovely," Mrs. Szalagy said to Louisa. "And I don't believe any of those rumors about you being pregnant."

Beyond Mrs. Szalagy was Aunt Ruth with cousins Margaret and Mary, beyond Margaret and Mary was Uncle Bill. And standing in front of the fireplace was the justice of the peace and Pete. Alongside Pete stood the best man . . . Kurt. Kurt was wearing his black-knit watch cap pulled low over his ears. He hadn't shaved and a cigarette dangled precariously from his lower lip. An inch-long ash dropped off the end of his cigarette and fell onto his filthy sweatshirt. Louisa and her father stopped in front of Pete and Kurt, and Louisa's father took her veil in hand.

"Um, wait a minute," Louisa said. "I don't think I want to marry Kurt."

"You're not marrying Kurt," her father replied. "You're marrying Pete."

"Yes, but Kurt is part of the deal. He'll come over to drink beer, and he'll leave grease spots on the wall behind the couch."

Louisa sighed. So, there it was . . . her wedding. Grim, she thought. Very grim.

Pete's door was unlocked. She let herself in and plodded up the stairs.

Pete was slouched in a chair. He tipped his head back to look at her through half-closed eyes.

"I've got supper," Louisa said. She took a closer look at him. "You look terrible."

"Good. I'd hate to think I could feel this lousy and not have anybody notice."

She put her hand to his forehead. "You feel feverish."

"Don't say that. I can't have a fever. I refuse."

"You seemed healthy enough when I left this morning."

"It's all your fault," he said. "You made me go to the zoo in the rain, and then you wore me out with your constant demands for my sexual services." He groaned. "Now I have a cold. I haven't had a cold in nine years."

"Poor baby."

"My throat is scratchy, and my eyes are watering, and I keep sneezing." He looked over at her. "Am I making any points, here? Do you want to marry me out of pity?"

"I don't do pity marriages."

"This cold is worthless."

"Not totally," she told him. "I'd be willing to fork over a reasonable amount of sympathy."

"Would you be willing to fork it over in California? I got a call from the coast this afternoon. They're starting production, and I need to be there."

Louisa felt her heart stop for a fraction of a second. "You never said anything about leaving for California."

"I guess it just never came up. I should have been there weeks ago, but I didn't want to take off until the pig thing was resolved."

"When are you going?"

"Tomorrow."

"*Tomorrow?* Are you crazy? You can't go to-morrow. Look at you—you're sick."

"I'll take some cold pills. I'll be fine."

"How long will you be gone?"

"Couple months, at least. First, they'll shoot the location scenes in downtown L.A., then they'll do the interiors in Burbank."

She felt as if somebody had just hit her in the face with a board. She didn't want to marry him, but she didn't want to lose him, either. The truth was, she'd gotten used to him. Now he was going to up and fly away. "Men!" she said.

"You're upset."

She had her arms crossed over her chest, and she was pacing. "Hell no. I'm not upset. What would I be upset about?"

"You're gonna miss me."

"Maybe a little."

"You could come with me."

He was serious! "Good Lord," she said, "you're giving me twelve hours' notice to move to Cali-fornia!"

"That's not enough?"

"No!"

"Okay, so how much time do you need?"

She ran her hand through her hair. "I don't know . . . a year or two."

"I gotta go to bed," he said. "I gotta get some rest. I feel like death." He dragged himself up from the chair and shuffled off to the bedroom. "The plane leaves at seven-thirty tomorrow morning. I have a cab coming at six. You decide what you wanna do. There's a seat reserved on the plane if you want it."

He disappeared through the bedroom door, and Louisa heard him flop onto the bed. She followed him in and removed his shoes. "Can I get you anything. Some soup or tea?"

"A gun," he said. "Get me a gun and shoot me."

She drew the quilt over him. "You'll feel better tomorrow."

"You really think so?" he asked hopefully.

"No," she said. "You'll probably feel worse."

Ten

At six the next morning, Louisa heard Pete stomp down the stairs. All night long she'd wrestled with her feelings, and she still hadn't reached a conclusion. He knocked on her door, and she hesitated in answering. She sat hunched in her bed, covers pulled up to her chin, not sure what she should say to him. He knocked again, she sighed and went to the door.

"Morning," he said, his face stiffening at the sight of her in her nightgown. "Looks like I'm going alone." He had two suitcases, a portable PC, and Spike in a cat carrier. The cab was waiting at the curb.

"I'm sorry," Louisa said. "I can't."

He gave her a slip of paper. "If you change your mind, this is my address. There's a map on the back, and my phone number."

"How's your cold?"

"I'll live."

They both stared down at their feet. The silence was awkward. Spike yowled, and the cabdriver beeped his horn. Pete said something rude in reply.

"Call me," Louisa said.

"Sure."

She adjusted his scarf. "Take care of yourself."

"I will."

"Will you be coming back to Washington?"

"Of course I'll be coming back to Washington," he said. "I live here."

"Gosh," Louisa said, "no need to get cranky about it."

"No need to get cranky?" His voice rose an octave. "I asked you to marry me, and you turned me down as if I were yesterday's potatoes! And besides, I have a cold. People are supposed to be cranky when they have a cold." He took a wad of tissues from his pocket and blew his nose. "If you have problems with the apartment, call the property manager. You have his number." He gave her a set of keys. "Keys to my apartment and keys to the Porsche. The Porsche is garaged on the street behind us. The number is on the paper I gave you. Use the car if you want." The cabdriver leaned on his horn. "I have to go," Pete said to Louisa.

She bit down on her lower lip to keep it from trembling. "I hate good-byes."

"The plane doesn't leave until seven-thirty. There's still time to change your mind."

She shook her head.

He sneezed twice and blew his nose again. He picked up the cat carrier and trudged down the steps to the cab.

Louisa raised her hand to wave, but he never looked back. He was hurt and angry, she thought. She leaned her head against the doorjamb and watched the cab drive away. "I can't go with you," she said. "I'm not a California person. I don't tan well, I fall asleep on one glass of wine, I don't know how to give fake kisses. What would I do if I got invited to a barbecue at Paul Simon's house?"

A blast of freezing air swirled up her nightgown, reminding her that she was standing on the porch. She shivered, as much from gloom as from cold, then firmly closed the door and retreated back to her warm bed.

She'd always imagined a marriage as being comfortably boring. It was a place to feel safe. A place to relax. She shook her head sadly. She'd never be able to relax in California. To begin with there were all those starlets named Bambi. She peeked under the covers at her flannel-wrapped body. She'd have to get breast implants and liposuctioned if she wanted to compete with Bambi. She'd need lip augmentation to give herself that pouty look, and Mr. Ray's hair weave, and rhinoplasty, and a full set of caps.

It took an hour and a half to go through all of the reasons why she couldn't go to California. She ran out of reasons just as the paper thunked against the front door, so she threw the covers aside and swung her legs out of bed. She stuffed her feet into her slippers, belted her robe around her, and set forth to enjoy her morning ritual. She made the coffee, tuned in to NPR, read the paper, and ate an English muffin as a special treat.

At eight-thirty she dressed in sweats and sneakers and began cleaning her house. She vacuumed, polished, scrubbed, and scoured until every surface was shiny clean. She cleaned the toaster, the range hood, the oven, and the refrigerator. She cleaned her closets, rearranged her drawers, and put down her new shelf paper. She cleaned until eleven-thirty at night.

At eleven-thirty she stood in front of her full-length mirror and assessed her thighs. They didn't need liposuction, but they weren't up to Bambi's standards, either. Louisa burst into tears and went to bed. Hormones, she told herself. She was just suffering a small endocrine imbalance. She was sure she'd wake up the following morning feeling peachy dandy.

The second day she did the laundry. She ironed all the sheets, pillowcases, and towels. She ironed her underwear, her jeans, and her T-shirts. She polished the leaves on her plants, scoured her garbage can, and tried to wash her car, but the water kept freezing. She told herself she was doing all of these things because the following week she was going to do serious job hunting. Once she went back to work for real she wouldn't have time to scrub the grout with a toothbrush, she told herself. Deep down inside, she knew better. She'd known the moment the cab had disappeared from view. Maybe she'd even known sooner than that. Maybe she'd always known. She was going to go to California. She wasn't sure what she'd do after she got there, but she was going all the same. And before she stepped off into the unknown, she'd needed to set her life in order.

She baked a double batch of chocolate chip cookies and ate half of them for supper. She put the rest of the cookies in a straw basket, wrapped it in cellophane, and tied the cellophane together at the top with a yellow ribbon. She packed two small suitcases with summery clothes and set them beside the front door. She hadn't canceled her paper or emptied her refrigerator. She wasn't sure how long she'd be gone. She painted her nails in a bright peach shade to bolster her self-confidence and went to bed.

Louisa's mother looked at the newly polished houseplants sitting in her foyer, at the little black car sitting in her driveway, and at her daughter, dressed in a lemon-yellow linen suit. "Let me get this straight," her mother said, holding the basket of cookies. "You're going to California."

"Yes."

"This is very sudden."

"It's something I have to do," Louisa said.

"Like when you were seven and you had to see how a bathroom scale worked so you took ours apart? And when you were nine you had to see if you could climb to the top of the Szalagy's oak tree, and the fire department had to come get you down?"

"Yup. Just like that."

"I don't suppose this has anything to do with your screenwriter friend?"

Grandma Brannigan stood in the kitchen doorway. "You aren't going to go out there and live in sin, are you? You know what they say about giving out free samples, don't you?"

"He's asked me to marry him," Louisa said.

"He don't look like the marrying kind to me," Grandma Brannigan said. "He's got a ponytail, for one thing. What kind of man wears a ponytail? And I saw that flashy car he drives. You know what they say about men who drive them fast cars. They say their body parts aren't all what they should be."

Louisa handed her mother a set of keys. "These are for my car and my house. I'll call tomorrow and let you know where I'm staying."

Grandma Brannigan made a disgusted sound with her tongue. "You hear that, Katherine? She don't even know where she's going to be staying. I wouldn't let a daughter of mine go off like that."

Louisa's mother sighed. "She's thirty years old, for goodness sakes."

Grandma Brannigan looked confused. "How'd she turn out to be so old?"

Louisa smiled and hugged her grandmother. "I'll see you when I get back. Try to behave yourself."

"Are you going to marry him?" Louisa's mother asked.

Louisa took a moment to answer. "I don't know."

She walked to the rental car counter at Los Angeles airport with shaky legs—but also with a sense of accomplishment. The plane hadn't fallen out of the sky ahead of time, she hadn't lost control of her body functions and embarrassed herself, and she'd barely whimpered on takeoff and landing. She'd even looked out the window once. It took two tries before she managed to sign her name to the rental agreement. "I'm not a good flier," she explained to the girl behind the counter. "I get a little nervous."

"No kidding." The girl gave Louisa a set of keys. "Flying's the easy part. Wait'll you try to drive yourself out of this airport."

An hour later, Louisa was on Route 101, passing through Ventura. The air was warm and the sky was dusky. The Pacific Ocean rolled away to her left, as far as the eye could see. She was driving a new little compact, and she was feeling like Ferdinand Magellan.

California was more dust and dirt than she'd imagined. There were splotches of green where lawns had been watered, but the gentle hills that lay to the east were parched and sun bleached. Vistas were open, buildings were low. Santa Barbara felt Spanish and upscale with its stucco buildings and red-tiled roofs. She rolled through town and headed east into Santa Barbara County, following Pete's map. Fields were colored with wild poppies and lupine, and the sky melted into the land in a lavender haze as the sun sank lower.

She quickly realized she would never have found Pete without the map. Small roads snaked off into darkening woods. There were no names to the roads, and she suspected they were private drives. She passed several avocado orchards and an Arabian horse farm and hit another section of woods and little feeder roads. She scrupulously counted off the dirt roads and turned right where the map indicated.

After an eighth of a mile she came to an adobe gate house. The gate was open, and Louisa continued driving. Woods gave way to wild grasses, the road smoothed into a flawless ribbon of crushed yellow stone, and on a rise ahead of her she could see another adobe house. It was a sprawling ranch, capped in red tile, anchored by a thick profusion of flowers. It wasn't especially large—two or three bedrooms, she guessed. She held her breath and prayed she was at the right house. He stomach settled when she saw Spike sprawled on the front porch.

She felt a moment's panic that Pete might not be alone or that he might have changed his mind. He hadn't called as he'd promised, and neither had she. She'd been afraid the conversation might not go exactly right, and she'd chicken out. Now she wished she'd at least phoned from the airport and warned him. She pushed the panic away and parked in the circular drive. She straightened her suit and marched up to the front door.

Pete answered on the second knock. He was wearing shorts and a gray T-shirt with cough syrup spilled down the front. "Oh no," he said. "Not you."

The panic came back in a hot wave that hit her square in the chest. "I should have called."

He sneezed. "Stand back. I'm contaminated. I thing I'b god the flu." He sneezed again and wiped his nose with the bottom of his T-shirt. "Sorry," he said, "I'b run oud of tissues."

"Is anyone taking care of you? You have a housekeeper?"

"Jus' me and Spike."

Louisa smiled. He needed her. The Hollywood Husband was out of tissues. No one was making him chicken soup or custard. No one was listening to him complain about how lousy he felt. "Why didn't you call?"

"I'b been sick!" he wailed.

She looked around. This house was much more spacious than his Washington apartment. The furniture was southwestern. The floor was wide pine, and the aroma of flowers and baked grass drifted through the open patio door.

He sniffed, and she gave him some tissues from her purse. "Stay right here," she said. "I'll get you some toilet paper."

"Don't have any," he said sadly. "Blew my nose in it all."

"Okay, how about napkins."

"None."

"Paper towels?"

"All gone." He flopped in a chair. "I'b a failure, Lou. I'b no gud ad being sick."

"How much of that syrup have you had?"

"Nod enough. I ran oud, so I switched to brandy."

"Oh boy."

"And I'be been lonely, Lou. I'b missed you."

"I've missed you too."

"Did you come to marry me?"

"I'm thinking about it."

"I'b glad," he said. "I'b waited a long time for you. Years and years." His eyes dropped closed, and he sighed. "I lub you."

Two weeks later she was still thinking about marriage. She was thinking that it might not be so bad. Paul Simon hadn't called with a barbecue invitation, and she hadn't met any women named Bambi. Not that it mattered, she told herself, because she was the new Lou, and she could handle whatever.

She was sitting on the front porch with Spike, and she was waiting for Pete to come home from the day's shoot. "No different from working at AT&T or General Dynamics," Louisa said to Spike. "He goes out in the morning, and he comes home in the evening, just like any other man."

A limo cruised by the gate house and began the climb to the top of the hill. It stopped in front of Louisa, and Pete got out, holding his lap-top and the latest version of the script. He closed the door, and the limo took off down the hill. "Well, another day at the salt mines," Pete said.

Okay, so maybe he wasn't exactly like any other man, Louisa conceded.

He set the computer on the porch and pulled Louisa to her feet, kissing her fiercely, needing to make up for the time away from her. Immediately, he was hard and hungry, almost out of control. He stripped her shirt over her head, tugged at the closure on her bra, and her breasts tumbled out into his hands.

Louisa gasped. "Good Lord, not on the front lawn!"

He hooked his thumb into the elastic waistband of her shorts and peeled them over her hips, exposing her flat stomach and dark triangle of curls.

She reached for the shorts, but he'd been too quick. They were on the ground. She turned for the privacy of the house and found he was blocking her way. He kissed her again, pulling her tight against him, his fingers gripping the undersides of her cheeks. He dropped to his knees and took his mouth to her.

"This is crazy," she said, barely able to form the words, barely able to think for the sensations his mouth was causing. "Suppose someone's in the woods? Or walking along the hilltop?"

His smile was dark and feral. "Then they would see you. They'd hear you moan when my tongue touched you. They'd watch while you spread your legs and took me in." He pulled her down onto the grass, and ran his fingers over the part of her that was slick and inviting. "Would you like to be watched?"

"Well, actually . . . no."

"Suppose you were the person in the woods, and you happened upon two people in the throes of passion. Would you close your eyes? Or would you enjoy the show?"

She had to think longer about that, and while she was thinking Pete cleverly found the perfect spot. He teased her until she was panting and writhing under his hand. "Have you decided yet?" he asked her.

Her voice was thick when she answered. "What was the question?"

He laughed and kissed her . . . slowly. Everywhere. She begged for release, and he gave it to her. Then he stripped and took her on the front lawn.

It was almost dark when they were done, and the air was deliciously cool on Louisa's flushed skin. "Pervert," Louisa said.

He eased his weight from her. "A man's gotta do what a man's gotta do."

"Mmmm."

"You seemed to like it."

"I have to admit, doing it on the lawn held a certain allure, but I'm starting to feel a little weird."

"Takes some getting used to," he said.

"You've done this a lot?"

"No. But I've thought about it a lot. Mostly on the way home in the limo." He raised his head and sniffed. "I smell meat loaf."

"It's dinner."

"You made meat loaf for dinner?" He got to his feet and took her with him. "If I'd know there was meat loaf in the oven, I never would have bothered with sex."

The cherry blossoms were blooming when Pete and Louisa returned to Washington. They stood on the front porch of the house on 27th Street, suitcases stacked at their feet, and they looked at the two front doors.

"We have sort of an odd problem here," Pete said. "It looks to me like we're at a crossroads in our relationship."

Louisa steeled herself to a nervous flutter in her stomach. He hadn't mentioned marriage for a month and a half, and she was scared to broach the subject. She opted for the safe, cowardly route. "I suppose we should move back into our own apartments."

"Is that what you want?"

She could hear the wounded surprise in his voice and secretly rejoiced. The idea of living separately was just as abhorent to him as it was to her. In the past two months she'd come to appreciate Pete's easy-going ways. His casual. attitude about possessions and routine had made him a comfortable housemate. She thought it strange that those traits she'd originally hated in him were the very things she now found most appealing. And the little rituals of peace and solitude that had once been so important, now seemed sterile and distasteful. She enjoyed sharing her paper and her morning coffee. And she loved him. Lord, how she loved him.

"Well?" Pete asked.

"I'm thinking."

He sighed and looked heavenward for patience. "Take your time."

"You play your cards right, and I might consider marrying you."

He flashed her a wide smile. "I knew you'd come around. What finally clinched it? Was it my charm? My superior intelligence? My studly butt?"

She shook her head. "It was your ventilation system."

"You mean you're marrying me because my apartment smells better than yours?"

"There's more. Remember when you asked me what women wanted from a marriage and I said undying devotion and a warm place to put cold feet?"

"Uh-huh."

"Can you guarantee me of both those things?"

"The undying devotion is easy. I don't know about the cold feet. Which warm place did you have in mind?"

"You'll never change," she said. "Your mind is always in the gutter."

"It's my birthright."

"It would have to be a church wedding," Louisa said.

"Of course."

"And Kurt couldn't wear his watch cap and sweatshirt if he was best man."

"Kurt wouldn't be best man. My brother Chris would be best man." Pete saw the look of relief on her face. Understandable, he thought. And because he didn't want to ruin the moment for her, he didn't have the heart to tell her about Chris. Besides, after Kurt, all those tattoos and the gold tooth might not seem so bad.

THE EDITOR'S CORNER

What a marvelously exciting time we'll have next month, when we celebrate LOVESWEPT's ninth anniversary! It was in May 1983 that the first LOVESWEPTs were published, and here we are, still going strong, still as committed as ever to bringing you only the best in category romances. Several of the authors who wrote books for us that first year have become *New York Times* bestselling authors, and many more are on the verge of achieving that prestigious distinction. We are proud to have played a part in their accomplishments, and we will continue to bring you the stars of today—and tomorrow. Of course, none of this would be possible without you, our readers, so we thank you very much for your continued support and loyalty.

We have plenty of great things in store for you throughout the next twelve months, but for now, let the celebration begin with May's lineup of six absolutely terrific LOVESWEPTs, each with a special anniversary message for you from the authors themselves.

Leading the list is Doris Parmett with **UNFINISHED BUSINESS,** LOVESWEPT #540. And there is definitely unfinished business between Jim Davis and Marybeth Wynston. He lit the fuse of her desire in college but never understood how much she wanted independence. Now, years later, fate plays matchmaker and brings them together once more when his father and her mother start dating. Doris's talent really shines in this delightful tale of love between two couples.

In **CHILD BRIDE,** LOVESWEPT #541, Suzanne Forster creates her toughest, sexiest renegade hero yet. Modern-day bounty hunter Chase Beaudine rides the Wyoming badlands and catches his prey with a lightning whip. He's ready for anything—except Annie Wells, who claims they were wedded to each other five years ago when he was in South America on a rescue mission. To make him believe her, Annie will use the most daring—and passionate—

moves. This story sizzles with Suzanne's brand of stunning sensuality.

Once more Mary Kay McComas serves up a romance filled with emotion and fun—**SWEET DREAMIN' BABY,** LOVESWEPT #542. In the small town where Bryce LaSalle lives, newcomers always arouse curiosity. But when Ellis Johnson arrives, she arouses more than that in him. He tells himself he only wants to protect and care for the beautiful stranger who's obviously in trouble, but he soon finds he can do nothing less than love her forever. With her inimitable style, Mary Kay will have you giggling, sighing, even shedding a tear as you read this sure-to-please romance.

Please give a rousing welcome to newcomer Susan Connell and her first LOVESWEPT, **GLORY GIRL,** #543. In this marvelous novel, Evan Jamieson doesn't realize that his reclusive next-door neighbor for the summer is model Holly Hamilton, the unwilling subject of a racy poster for Glory Girl products. Evan only knows she's a mysterious beauty in hiding, one he's determined to lure out into the open—and into his arms. This love story will bring out the romantic in all of you and have you looking forward to Susan's next LOVESWEPT.

Joyce Anglin, who won a Waldenbooks award for First Time Author in a series, returns to LOVESWEPT with **OLD DEVIL MOON,** #544. Serious, goal-oriented Kendra Davis doesn't know the first thing about having fun, until she goes on her first vacation in years and meets dashing Mac O'Conner. Then there's magic in the air as Mac shows Kendra that life is for the living . . . and lips are made for kissing. But could she believe that he'd want her forever? Welcome back, Joyce!

Rounding the lineup in a big way is **T.S., I LOVE YOU,** LOVESWEPT #545, by Theresa Gladden. This emotionally vivid story captures that indefinable quality that makes a LOVESWEPT romance truly special. Heroine T. S. Winslow never forgot the boy who rescued her when she was a teenage runaway, the boy who was her first love.

Now, sixteen years later, circumstances have brought them together again, but old sorrows have made Logan Hunter vow never to give his heart. Theresa handles this tender story beautifully!

Look for four spectacular books on sale this month from FANFARE. First, **THE GOLDEN BARBARIAN,** by best-selling author Iris Johansen—here at last is the long-awaited historical prequel to the LOVESWEPT romances created by Iris about the dazzling world of Sedikhan. A sweeping novel set against the savage splendor of the desert, this is a stunningly sensual tale of passion and love between a princess and a sheik, two of the "founders" of Sedikhan. *Romantic Times* calls **THE GOLDEN BARBARIAN** ". . . an exciting tale . . . The sizzling tension . . . is the stuff which leaves an indelible mark on the heart." *Rendezvous* described it as ". . . a remarkable story you won't want to miss."

Critically acclaimed author Gloria Goldreich will touch your heart with **MOTHERS,** a powerful, moving portrait of two couples whose lives become intertwined through surrogate motherhood. What an eloquent and poignant tale about family, friendship, love, and the promise of new life.

LUCKY'S LADY, by ever-popular LOVESWEPT author Tami Hoag, is now available in paperback and is a must read! Those of you who fell in love with Remy Doucet in **RESTLESS HEART** will lose your heart once more to his brother, for bad-boy Cajun Lucky Doucet is one rough and rugged man of the bayou. And when he takes elegant Serena Sheridan through a Louisiana swamp to find her grandfather, they generate what *Romantic Times* has described as "enough steam heat to fog up any reader's glasses."

Finally, immensely talented Susan Bowden delivers a thrilling historical romance in **TOUCHED BY THORNS.** When a high-born beauty determined to reclaim her heritage strikes a marriage bargain with a daring Irish soldier, she never expects to succumb to his love, a love that would deny the English crown, and a deadly conspiracy.

And you can get these four terrific books only from FANFARE, where you'll find the best in women's fiction.

Also on sale this month in the Doubleday hardcover edition is **INTIMATE STRANGERS** by Alexandra Thorne. In this gripping contemporary novel, Jade Howard will slip into a flame-colored dress—and awake in another time, in another woman's life, in her home . . . and with her husband. Thoroughly absorbing, absolutely riveting!

Happy reading!

With warmest wishes,

Nita Taublib

Nita Taublib
Associate Publisher
FANFARE and LOVESWEPT